## *The raging brown water hurled Cady downstream,*

toward James's wagon. Her head kept ducking under and then bobbing up again as she sputtered and tried to scream. James wasn't even sure she saw him, but he stretched out over the water as far as he could.

"Cady, take my hand!" James shouted.

But she went under and swept right past him.

"Cady!" he screamed.

Her yellow hair broke the surface some yards downstream.

"I'm coming, Cady! Hang on!" James went to dive out of the wagon, but his ma gripped his leg.

"Don't, Jamie!" she pleaded.

"She's gonna drown!" James shot Jeremy a look, and his brother took Ma gently by the shoulders. She eased back into his grasp and released James's leg.

He tumbled into the river.

**Don't miss the next two books in this exciting western trilogy:**

*Along the Dangerous Trail*

*Over the Rugged Mountain*

**coming soon from HarperPaperbacks!**

# ACROSS THE WILD RIVER

## BILL GUTMAN

# HarperPaperbacks
*A Division of* HarperCollins*Publishers*

This is a work of fiction. The characters, incidents, and
dialogues are products of the author's imagination and are not
to be construed as real. Any resemblance to actual events or
persons, living or dead, is entirely coincidental.

HarperPaperbacks  *A Division of* HarperCollins*Publishers*
10 East 53rd Street, New York, N.Y. 10022

Produced by Daniel Weiss Associates, Inc., 33 West 17th
Street, New York, New York 10011.

First printing: September, 1993

Printed in the United States of America

HarperPaperbacks and colophon are trademarks of
HarperCollins*Publishers*

10 9 8 7 6 5 4 3 2 1

# ACROSS THE WILD RIVER

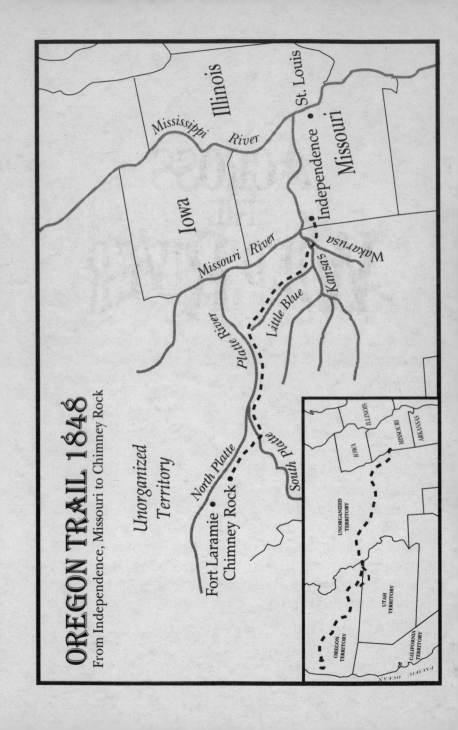

# ONE

## P. WHITFIELD, PROVISIONER

*Clip-clop, clip-clop, clip-clop.* James Gregg listened to the cheerful sound of his pa's chestnut draft horse trotting down the main street of Independence, Missouri. James was sitting next to his pa on the front board of the wagon. On the other side sat Jeremy, James's older brother.

The Gregg family had arrived in Independence only three days before. Ma and Elizabeth, James's younger sister, were back at the wagon camp outside of town. The Greggs had come all the way from Pennsylvania.

"Whoa, Mackie," Pa said, pulling back gently on the reins. He gave a low shushing sound and Mackie came to a halt, shaking his mane and huffing through his bit. They were in front of a wide, two-story wooden building. A sign over the door said P. WHITFIELD, PROVISIONER in large black letters. Underneath, in smaller letters, was *Established 1847*.

James snickered at the sign. That was just last year. "Why are we stopping here?" he asked his pa.

"I need to pick up some buckshot," Pa said. "And your mother asked me to get her a little extra flour. We have to be prepared for the trip ahead." The Greggs were joining a wagon train that would be leaving for Oregon the next day. The trip would take about five months. "You boys want to come inside the store with me?"

"No, sir," Jeremy muttered. He pulled his hat down low over his eyes and stared straight ahead. "I'm not interested."

"All right, then," Pa said, running his hand over his beard. "You can stay here and watch Mackie." He turned to James. "How about you, Jamie? You interested?"

"Sure, Pa," James said. "I'll go with you." He hopped off the wagon while Pa handed the reins to Jeremy.

"Mackie's not used to crowds," Pa said. "If he starts to shy, just tug on the reins and—"

"I know how to handle a horse," Jeremy said sharply. His hat was pulled so low, James couldn't see his eyes at all.

"Right," said Pa. "Well, come on, James. Let's go see Mr. Whitfield."

James and his pa walked across the dusty street

2

toward the low wooden sidewalk. It was raised up about one foot over the street below. James had never seen a sidewalk like it before.

"Do you think those boards can hold my weight?" he asked.

"I expect so," said Pa. "Though it's true you have been growing a lot lately. It's hard to believe you're twelve years old already. You must weigh nearly a hundred pounds by now."

"At least," James said. He stepped gingerly onto the sidewalk. It held. He jumped up and down a few times. "I guess it's safe," he announced.

"Thanks for testing it," Pa said, then stepped onto the sidewalk himself.

They went through the big open doorway to P. Whitfield, Provisioner. James had never seen so many different things together in one place before. Everywhere he looked, there were piles of cloth, barrels of flour, and sacks of seed. Mr. Whitfield sold iron tools of all kinds, clothing, fishhooks, candles, stoves, even spare wooden wagon wheels and their iron rims—everything James could think of that a body might need on the long trek west.

James's eyes fell upon the row of shiny, long black rifles in the case behind the back counter.

"I sure would like to shoot one of those," he whispered. "I bet I could get me a fine rabbit."

"We'll be hunting bigger game than rabbit, son," said his pa. He was scooping flour out of a large barrel into a cloth sack. "Out west there's buffalo that're as big as Mackie."

"Sakes," said James. "Can I go on the buffalo hunts?"

"I'm afraid you're too young yet. But I'm depending on you to look after your mother and Elizabeth. I can trust you, can't I?" Pa gave him a serious look as he measured shot into another sack.

"'Course," said James, though he was thinking he'd rather be shooting at buffalo than chasing after a little sister.

Pa took his shot and flour to the back counter for weighing. Mr. Whitfield dropped the sack of flour onto a large brass platform on the floor. Behind the platform was a circular scale at the top of a five-foot pole. The needle pointed to seventy-three pounds. Then Mr. Whitfield weighed the shot. Six pounds.

"Hop on up there, Jamie," Pa said, pointing to the brass platform. "Let's see how much you weigh."

James glanced at Mr. Whitfield, who smiled and nodded, and then stepped onto the platform. The needle pointed to ninety-nine pounds.

"Aw," said James. "Not even a hundred."

"Hold still," said Pa. He reached into the sack and drew out a fistful of shot. He poured them into James's overalls pocket. The needle edged up to one hundred.

James brightened. "I won't tell if you won't."

# TWO

## THE FIRST RUNAWAY

Pa paid for the provisions, and he and James left the store. Across the street, Mackie nervously flicked his mane and pawed at the ground. He didn't like all the noises in town. Jeremy was talking with a young man. James recognized him as the third mate from the ferry they'd taken up the Missouri from St. Louis.

"Think you can carry these to the wagon?" Pa asked James.

"Sure," James replied, taking the heavy sacks.

"I have to run another errand," Pa said. "I'll just be a minute."

James lugged the heavy sacks across the dusty street. He struggled to push the seventy-three-pound sack of flour over the side of the wagon.

Jeremy looked over his shoulder at his brother, then turned and whispered something to the third mate. The man nodded and scurried away.

"Howdy to you too, Jamie," James muttered to himself as the sack finally fell into the wagon. He leaned against the side of a building and took a look around.

There were people everywhere. James wondered how many of them were with the wagon train. He didn't think Independence could always be this crowded. Many of them were loading wagons and mules. They were carrying sacks of flour, sugar, salt, and coffee. They must be emigrants too, he decided.

James was fascinated by all the activity. There was nothing like this where he was from. Laughter and loud voices burst through the doors of a saloon. A constant clanging of hammers on iron came from the many blacksmith shops. At least he was familiar with this sound—he had often helped his father shoe Mackie back home.

"What a boring old town, huh?" came a voice.

James turned and saw a boy about the same age as himself. The boy was pale and very thin. He was wearing a white shirt and trousers, not overalls like most of the men and boys in town.

"Boring?" James said. "I've never seen anything like it."

"Oh, well," said the boy, squinting up the street. "Guess it depends on where you're from."

James eyed the boy. He didn't seem a bad

sort. "I'm James Gregg," he offered.

"Scott Walker," said the boy.

"You live here?" James asked. Maybe that was why he thought Independence was boring. They ambled down the sidewalk, though James kept a lookout for his pa, who would be returning soon.

"No," said Scott. "We're here to join a wagon train."

"The Stewart train?"

"That's the one," Scott said. "You gonna be on it too?"

"Yep. All the way to Oregon. We come from Pennsylvania."

"I'm from Pennsylvania too!" Scott smiled broadly. "Put'er there." He held out his hand, and the boys shook. "My father had a hardware store in Philadelphia," Scott said.

James knew that Philadelphia was a big city. No wonder Scott wasn't impressed with Independence. "We had a farm outside Franklin," James said. Before Independence, Franklin had been the liveliest town James had ever seen. "They say the best farmland in the whole country is in Oregon. And the government is just *giving* it away!"

It was true. Any man with the gumption could go to Oregon and stake a claim of three hundred twenty acres, or half a square mile. If he had a wife, he could claim six hundred forty acres!

"The farmland is rich," Scott allowed. "But we

7

aren't looking to farm. Father says he's going to have the biggest hardware store in all of Oregon."

James was glad he had met someone his own age. He hadn't had anyone to talk to except sour old Jeremy and pesky Elizabeth since they'd left the farm a month ago. Now he felt like he was finally going to have some fun.

But just then a loud voice rang out. "Scott Walker! You said you were gonna wait for me. Wait till Mother hears what you did."

James turned to see a tall, gangly girl striding toward them.

"Who's that?" James whispered.

"My sister, Cady," said Scott. He rolled his eyes.

Now that he had a better look at her, James could tell she was Scott's sister. But while Scott was thin and frail, Cady Walker was healthy, to say the least. She looked like she was all bone and muscle.

Cady had dirty-blond hair that hung loosely over her shoulders, and a long face like her brother's. Light brown freckles were sprinkled across the bridge of her nose. She seemed to be studying James as closely as he was studying her.

Cady dug into the side pocket of her dress, then popped a piece of rock candy into her mouth.

"I'd give you some," she said to the two boys, "but not after Scott left me like that."

"It was my fault," James said, even if that wasn't

8

quite the truth. "We got to talking. My name's James Gregg."

"I'm Cady," she said. "And Scott shouldn't have wandered away from me, no matter what. Mother told us to stick together."

"Well, I'm sorry," said Scott. "But you're here now."

"Hmph," said Cady. Still, she handed Scott and James each a small piece of candy.

When they started walking again, Scott began to cough so hard that he doubled over. James and Cady stopped. Finally he took a deep breath and said, "I'm all right. Just keep walking."

James and Cady did as he said.

"I turned thirteen last January," Scott said. "My father thinks the trip to Oregon will make a man of me."

James looked over at Scott. He found it hard to believe that Scott was older than he was.

"I'm eleven," said Cady.

"That puts me right in the middle," James said.

"You got any brothers or sisters?" Scott asked.

"One of each," James said. "Jeremy's fifteen. That's him on the wagon." He pointed up the street. Jeremy was leaning back and had his hat over his face. He looked to be asleep. "And my little sister, Elizabeth, is six. She's all right, though sometimes she's a handful. Jeremy treats me like a baby."

"I'm glad I don't have a big brother," said Scott.

9

"You just have a sister who's bigger," teased Cady.

Scott rolled his eyes again and slapped her gently on the arm. But James saw it was true—Cady was bigger than Scott.

Suddenly a loud shot rang out, and James saw a man stagger through the swinging double doors of the saloon. The man was clutching his stomach and stumbling down the sidewalk. He fell on his side. The front of his overalls was stained with blood. Cady screamed, and James and Scott grabbed her and pulled her back. The man opened his eyes and moaned softly.

James couldn't believe it—a real shooting right here, almost in front of his very eyes!

People were scattering in all directions. Horses in the street were neighing loudly and rearing at the shot while mules brayed and kicked out behind them. Then, through the wild commotion, a horse and wagon came charging down the street.

"Look out!" someone shouted. "Runaway horse!"

It was Mackie! James could see Jeremy's legs sticking up over the front board of the wagon. He must have dropped the reins and tumbled backward when Mackie started. Now Mackie was panicked and out of control. James knew a runaway horse in a crowded street was bound to get injured—and who knew what would happen to Jeremy? James started shouting and took a step toward Mackie, but he

10

knew there was no way he'd be able to stop him.

Then James saw a figure dart out of Mr. Whit-field's store. It was a young man. He spotted the wagon and bolted toward the runaway horse. When he was close enough, he leaped through the air and threw both arms around Mackie's neck.

For a moment it didn't look as if the horse would stop.

"He's gonna be trampled!" Scott shouted.

"No, look!" James said.

The young man dug his heels into the dusty road.

"Whoa, boy, whoa!" he said to the horse. "Whoa, boy, whoa!"

James could tell the man knew what he was doing. He dug his heels harder into the road and kept yelling "Whoa!" Once Mackie began to slow, James knew the man had him. Finally Mackie came to a halt. People in the street began to cheer. So did James, Scott, and Cady.

James ran over to the crowd gathered around the young man. "That was the bravest thing I ever saw!" he said.

"Aw, it was nothing," the young man said with a drawl, brushing the dust off his trousers and blue work shirt. He didn't look much older than Jeremy. "Horse got a little excited by the shot, 's all."

"I'd have had him reined in in a second," Jeremy said from the wagon. He reached for his hat, which had tumbled behind the sacks of flour and shot.

11

"I'm sure you would've," came a deep, stern voice, "if you hadn't been sprawled out like a weevil on its back."

James turned and saw his pa, then snorted.

Pa glared at James. "And don't you laugh, boy."

"No, sir," said James.

Jeremy climbed sheepishly out of the wagon.

"Didn't I tell you to mind Mackie while I was gone?" Pa asked Jeremy.

"Yes, sir," Jeremy mumbled.

"I'll see to you later." Pa turned to the young man, pumped his hand, and smiled. "I want to thank you," he said. "You saved my horse and my wagon." He shot Jeremy a look. "Not to mention my boy. I'm obliged. How can I pay you?"

The young man grinned and shook his head. "It was nothing," he said again. "I don't expect any kind of reward."

"Well, thank you kindly, anyway," said Pa. "Jeremy?"

"Yeah," said Jeremy, looking at his feet. "Thanks."

"Think nothing of it," the young man said modestly. Then he stepped into the crowd and was gone.

"That was the bravest thing I ever saw," James repeated.

"Me too," said Scott. He and Cady had just made their way through the crowd.

"Oh, it wasn't so—" Jeremy began, but Pa cut him off.

"Up on the wagon, boys, and let's get back to the women. We've had enough excitement for one day."

James waved to Scott and Cady as Pa giddapped Mackie. "See you on the train!" he shouted.

They waved back, and James settled in for the ride. Then he realized that, in all the hubbub over Mackie, he had never found out what happened to the bleeding man. They were passing the saloon he'd come out of. The man was gone. All that was left was a dark red smudge on the dusty wooden sidewalk.

# THREE

## THE TRAIN BOSS

"Am I hungry," said James, breathing in the aroma of cooking meat. "I could eat a whole buffalo myself."

His ma was humming to herself as she tended the big stewing kettle over the fire. "You'll have to get by with squirrel stew tonight, Jamie," she said.

James's ma was short and stocky, with a quick smile and a musical voice. She had bright blue eyes, with lines that crinkled up around them when she laughed. "Gifts from Mr. Sun and Mrs. Wind," she called them, but James thought of them as smile lines.

His pa sat nearby, resewing the seams on one of the tents to strengthen it. He was going through the supplies one last time. For times when they couldn't find game, the Greggs were carrying eggs packed in sacks of cornmeal; dried apples and pears; dried pumpkins; jerked beef and salt pork; and stacks and stacks of johnnycakes, which were hard, dried biscuits. Plus, of course, barrels of flour and cornmeal totaling three hundred pounds.

Pa had also brought the double-barreled shotgun, three rifles, five pounds of gunpowder, fifteen pounds of shot, twenty pounds of bullets, twelve boxes of percussion caps, two large sheaf knives, a hatchet, and an axe.

When Mackie bolted, back in Independence, Pa had been buying a last-minute item: a gross of fishhooks. Later, he told James they were valuable as barter with the Indians of the Snake River country, a thousand miles away. James admired the way his Pa could plan so far in advance. The box of fishhooks was now packed away at the bottom of the wagon.

All the wagons of the Stewart train were gathered just outside town in a broad, open field. The sun was setting, and James could see a dozen cook fires glowing in the distance.

"Did I have fun in town today," James said. "I made two friends and saw a man get shot to death!"

"Shot!" Ma exclaimed. She turned to her husband. "Sam, you didn't tell me about any shooting."

"Now, Amelia," he said, "the boy's exaggerating."

"What did he see, then?"

16

"I saw a man do this," James said. He clutched at his stomach and fell over.

"James Gregg!" Ma said. "That's not funny. And you stop snickering, too, Samuel!"

Pa wiped the smile off his face. "The boy didn't actually see the shooting—it happened inside the saloon."

"Saloon! What was he doing near a saloon?"

"Now, Amelia. He was just strolling by. And we don't know the man died. He was probably just wounded a little."

"Oh, he looked pretty wounded to me," James said.

Pa glared at him. "That's enough of that, son."

Ma went back to stirring the stew, clucking to herself.

Then James asked his pa, "Do you think we'll see any real Indians on the trail?"

James had seen some Indians in Independence, but he didn't consider them "real" Indians. They were Sacs and Foxes from the reservation outside St. Joseph, and they were dressed like white people. James wanted to see Indians in feathers and war paint.

"I'm sure we'll see some," Pa answered. "Can't tell you how many."

"Samuel, don't scare the boy," said Ma.

"I'm not, Amelia. I'm just telling him the truth."

"I'm not scared," James said. "I can take care of

myself. Pa taught me how to shoot the Hawken last year."

"Stop talking about shooting and sit down for your dinner," Ma said. "But go fetch Jeremy and Elizabeth first. They're round abouts somewhere."

"Yes, Ma," James said. He walked around to the other side of the wagon, where he spotted six-year-old Elizabeth and quickly scooped her up.

"Put me down!" the little girl protested. Her long yellow braids swung to and fro as she shook her head.

"I will," said James, tucking her under his arm. "Right beside Ma."

Ma smiled at her son when he placed Elizabeth beside her. "Stay here now, Elizabeth," she said. "I don't want you wandering off again while James finds Jeremy."

"Be back in a minute," said James. He was really getting hungry and didn't want to waste any time rounding up his brother.

James cupped his hands and called for Jeremy. No response came. He started across the field, scanning it for his brother's face. At last he spotted Jeremy over by the train boss's wagon talking to the third mate from the ferry again. James trotted toward him, calling his name.

Jeremy spun around, and the other man slipped quietly into the shadows.

"What do you want?" Jeremy said sharply. He

was about a head taller than James. He had straight brown hair like his brother's, but he wore it longer. He'd told James that the girls liked it that way. James didn't see what that had to do with anything.

"Ma wants you to come to dinner," said James. "Who was that?" he asked, though he knew perfectly well.

"Nobody. Just some fellow asking me directions."

"Oh." James stood still for a moment.

"Well, let's get going, then," said Jeremy. "Dinner's getting cold."

As they walked across the campground, James said, "Aren't you excited about the trip? Pa said we might see us some real Indians."

"*You* might see some," said Jeremy. "But don't be so sure about 'us.'"

James said nothing. He didn't like the way Jeremy was talking.

"I know Missy can't live without me," Jeremy burst out. Missy was the girl he'd been sweet on back home. "It was awful when we said good-bye. It'd break your heart." He stopped and stared right at James, searching his face. "Don't ever make a pretty girl cry, Jamie."

"I won't," James said seriously. Why was his brother acting so peculiar? "I promise."

"I promised too," Jeremy said bitterly. "And I mean to keep that promise."

"Jeremy, what're you planning to do?" James

asked. He suddenly had a very bad feeling.

"Nothing!" Jeremy shouted. "And don't you say anything to Ma or Pa, either!" He spun on his heels and stalked off.

After dinner, several people from other wagons came calling. People and wagons had been gathering in Independence since early in the spring for the trip west. They had come from many different states; some had even traveled across the Atlantic to be here. All were looking for a better life.

Pa had explained to the family that the journey to Oregon would not be easy. The wagon train would be crossing rugged country. There would be hard work and real danger. Not everyone would make it. But with the trip about to begin at last, the mood in the camp was happy.

James could hear the sounds of harmonicas and fiddles cutting through the cool evening air. James took a deep breath and moved closer to the warm fire. His belly was full of good squirrel stew. He felt warm, safe, and hopeful.

Up strode a tall, thin man with a drooping yellow mustache and a hat with a long white feather in it. James recognized him as Colonel Thomas Stewart. He had been elected by the men in the train to serve as train boss. He would determine the route and set the schedule. The emigrants would be traveling through country where no government ruled. It was up to the train boss to settle disputes and see that justice was done.

James had heard that Colonel Stewart had been a hero at Palo Alto, one of the big battles of the Mexican War. The war had just ended in February.

The colonel was followed by a stout fellow dressed in well-worn buckskins. He was unshaven and, despite the wide grin on his face, looked about as friendly as a bear.

"Mr. Gregg," said the colonel to James's pa, "I want you to meet Pierre Delaroux. Mr. Delaroux is a hunter and trapper. He knows the Oregon country well. I've hired him to help the men hunt and to be our guide when we reach the Northwest."

The stocky man stepped forward and grasped Pa's hand. "How d'ya do?" he said, rocking back on his heels. A pair of bone-handled pistols hung from his belt, as well as a large knife. James thought this man could tell some really exciting stories about the wild country. He was a little scary, though. He appeared to be sizing James up for stew meat.

"Pleased to make your acquaintance, Mr. Delaroux," Pa said politely. He turned to Colonel Stewart. "Is everyone ready to roll?"

"I believe so," said the colonel. "We've had a few last-minute additions. Here's the contract. You'll be the last to sign."

"Can I see?" James asked.

Pa lowered the papers so James could look. At the top of the first page, in fancy handwriting, was the title, CONSTITUTION AND BYLAWS OF THE STEWART PARTY. Underneath was *Drafted this day, May 4, 1848.* Below that line were a bunch of numbered paragraphs filled up with long words that made no sense to James.

Pa murmured quietly as he read the document. The last page was filled with signatures:

| Name | No. in Party |
|------|------|
| *Col. Thomas Stewart* | *1* |
| *Pierre Delaroux* | *1* |
| *Caleb L. Batkin* | *5* |
| *Henry A. Jennington* | *3* |
| *William Gantry* | *1* |
| *Harlan Teague* | *6* |
| *Daniel Loughery* | *2* |
| *Piotr Skonecki* | *5* |
| *Chester Smoot* | *5* |
| *John Walker* | *4* |
| *Jenson Carver* | *1* |
| *Robert C. Connell* | *4* |
| *Ulf Sundstrom* | *6* |
| *Silas D. Moss* | *1* |
| *Eli Meacham* | *2* |
| *Patrick McElroy* | *6* |

At the bottom Pa added his own:

*Samuel J. Gregg* 5

Then he handed the papers back to Colonel Stewart.

"We roll at daybreak," said the colonel.

"We'll be there," Pa replied.

Colonel Stewart and Pierre Delaroux nodded, then strode off into the darkness.

James thought about Colonel Stewart, with his plumed hat and big blue coat, and Pierre Delaroux with his knife and buckskins. Then he looked at his pa. He was tall and wiry, and wore farmer's overalls. His reddish-brown beard and tanned, lined face weren't as impressive as Colonel Stewart's big golden mustache or Delaroux's wide, grizzly-bear face.

Then James remembered his father working the farm. He could drive a plow from sun to sun and never grow tired. James smiled. He bet old Delaroux couldn't do that.

James's thoughts were interrupted by a familiar voice. "There he is. Hey, James. James!"

Scott walked into the light of the fire, a smile on his thin face. Cady was a few feet behind him, along with their parents.

"Ma, Pa," said James. "This is Scott and Cady Walker. They're going to Oregon, too."

"Pleased to meet you," said James's ma.

Scott shook hands with James's folks, and Cady curtsied.

"This is my mother and father," Scott said.

John and Rebecca Walker introduced themselves to the Greggs. Mr. Walker was a big, barrel-chested man about two inches taller than James's pa. James could tell by the feel of his palm when he shook hands that Mr. Walker wasn't a farmer.

Mrs. Walker wore gold-rimmed glasses and a heavy black dress with a cameo pinned at the neck. She held herself stiffly, and didn't sit down when James's ma offered a spot on a crate.

"We're pretty new at all this," Mr. Walker said. "After I sold my hardware store, we had enough money to buy everything we needed for the trip right here in Independence."

"We built our wagon ourselves," said Pa. "All we have came straight off the farm. Even the young'uns."

"*Especially* the young'uns," Ma joked, and everyone laughed.

"Sounds like we're from opposite ends of the rope," Mr. Walker said. "Maybe we can help each other get through this. I'm handy with tools—wasn't in the hardware business for nothing, you might say."

"Why not," said Pa. "We're looking forward to claiming land in Oregon. They say the topsoil is six feet deep."

"Oh, we're not planning on farming," said Mr. Walker, holding up his hands. "That's too risky for me. I'm going to open up a hardware store."

"And I hope to teach Sunday school," Mrs. Walker announced, "as I did in Philadelphia. I'm sure God's word will be welcomed out West. Back home I read some awful stories—awful!—about frontier towns. Drunkenness, lawlessness . . . And don't even talk to me about those heathen Indians!"

*I won't*, James said to himself.

"Well," James's ma said, "we best be turning in. The Indians can wait, and we have a big day tomorrow."

That was certain. James said good-bye to Scott and Cady. He was looking forward to seeing them again on the trail. But right now he had to settle down for the night with his family.

# FOUR

## THE SECOND RUNAWAY

James couldn't sleep. He was excited about the coming journey. In his twelve years he had never seen much beyond the stone fences of the family farm. On the trip from Franklin to Independence, he'd hardly gotten off the ferries. The Greggs had gone down the Monongahela and Ohio rivers, then up the Mississippi a ways, and finally up the Missouri to Independence. James hadn't even gotten to see St. Louis, just below where the Missouri met the Mississippi. Now, finally, they would be traveling overland.

His father had told him Oregon was more than two thousand miles away. That was hard for him to imagine. He didn't think anything was that far off.

It was a warm night, and he decided to stretch his legs. Outside the tent, James looked up at the sky. It was clear, with bright stars everywhere. He wondered if the stars were two thousand miles away. He doubted it. Then he thought about Scott and Cady. He was glad he'd made some friends.

Something was troubling him, however. Jeremy. James knew his brother didn't want to go to Oregon. He'd made that clear enough. But Pa had told him the family should stick together. With the wagons rolling in the morning, James felt maybe he should try to talk to Jeremy. He wanted to tell him how much he was needed on the trip.

Jeremy was sleeping in the wagon. James didn't know how his brother could do it with all the things on board. He walked over to the back of the wagon and pulled aside the canvas flap. It was too dark to see anything.

"Jeremy," he said in a soft voice. "You awake?"

No answer.

"Jeremy," he repeated, this time a bit louder.

Still nothing. Quietly James climbed into the wagon. He groped around, chucking his shin on the edge of a wooden trunk. Finally he reached Jeremy's bedding. The blankets were rumpled but empty.

"Pa, get up!" James poked his head out the back of the wagon. "Jeremy's gone!"

Pa was at the wagon in seconds. Ma was right behind him.

"He isn't here," James said. "I don't know where he went."

"Oh, Sam, what're we gonna do?" Ma cried.

"We're gonna find him, that's what," said Pa.

"But the train rolls in the morning. What if he left camp?"

Pa sighed. "We'll find him," he told her. "That's all there is to it. James and I'll check the camp at sunup, then go to Independence and look."

James saw the troubled look on his ma's face.

"Amelia," Pa said gently. "We'll find him. But you know we've got to leave tomorrow, Jeremy or no Jeremy."

An hour before dawn Pa saddled Mackie and Corncob, the old nag, for James to ride. They quickly checked the wagon camp while the people made ready to leave. No one had seen Jeremy. Then they headed to Independence.

Pa rode at a quick canter. Mackie was a heavy draft horse and couldn't run very fast. Though Corncob was seventeen years old, she could easily keep up. James had been riding her since he could remember, and he handled her well.

The streets of Independence were nearly empty. They rode through town several times and saw nothing. Pa had just about given up hope.

"I wonder if there's a steamboat running downriver today," James said.

"Why do you say that?" Pa asked.

"I don't know. . . ." Should he tell Pa what he was thinking? Jeremy would say he was a tattler. But if he didn't say anything, he might never see Jeremy again. "I saw Jeremy talking to one of the ferry hands. I reckon maybe he's planning on working his way back to Franklin."

Pa gave James a quizzical look, then shouted, "Yah!" and heeled Mackie into a canter. "Let's go find your brother, Jamie!"

They rode the half mile to Independence Landing, where the steamboats came in on the Missouri. A few people were moving about, carrying crates and loading a wagon. Others sat around drinking coffee and smoking pipes. James and Pa dismounted and walked over to a small group of men.

"We're looking for my son," Pa said. "His name's Jeremy and he's fifteen years old. We think he might have come here to catch a steamship down-river."

"Look behind the smokehouse," one of the men said. "If I ain't mistaken, there was a young'un sleeping there earlier."

Pa thanked the man, and he and James walked to the small wooden building. The sweet aroma of smoking meat filled the air. James couldn't help thinking about how he'd missed breakfast this morning.

In back of the smokehouse they saw Jeremy curled beneath a blanket. He was just waking up.

"Howdy, Jeremy," said Pa. He spoke slowly and smiled. James smiled at his brother, too. He was glad to see him.

Jeremy had a hard look on his face. "I'm going back to Franklin and I'm not gonna change my mind," he said sourly.

"Come on, boy, let's take a walk," Pa ordered.

The sun was rising in the sky, and the air was warming rapidly. The three walked slowly down to the wharf and stood looking at the river for a few minutes.

"Jeremy, we need you to come with us," Pa said quietly. "We have difficult times ahead of us. If something should happen to me, I want you two boys to look after your mother and your sister."

"We never should've left Pennsylvania," Jeremy protested. "We were happy there. *I* was happy there. I had everything I wanted."

James knew he was talking about Missy.

"We've been through this before, son," said Pa. "I'm not gonna say it again. The wagons are leaving, and we have to get back. You're a man now, and I can't bring you by force. You have to choose." Pa turned to leave. "Come on, James, we have work to do."

James looked at his brother. "Jeremy . . ." he started. But he didn't know what to say. Pa was already mounting Mackie. James broke into a run and caught up to him. He swung himself up onto Corncob, then looked back.

"I'm not coming!" Jeremy yelled. "You hear me? I'm just not!"

Pa was silent the whole ride back to camp. James glanced over his shoulder several times, hoping to see Jeremy running after them. He couldn't believe he would be going to Oregon without his brother.

Most of the tents had already been struck by the time they got there. The animals had been brought in from their grazing area. Oxen were being yoked to wagons, ready to begin the long pull west.

James saw his ma struggling to yoke their family's two oxen. "Didn't you find him?" she asked Pa before he could even dismount.

"We found him," he said. "He refused to come with us. Says he's going back to Franklin."

"You just rode off?"

"I can't force the boy, Amelia," Pa said mildly. "He's a man now. He makes his choices."

"What's going to happen to him?" she asked. James could tell she was trying not to cry.

"Jeremy can take care of himself," James offered. "He'll make it home, and I bet he goes to live with Cousin Cara."

"James is right," Pa said. "Jeremy will be fine. We have to go on without him. Now, let's get to it.

Jamie, put Mackie and Corncob on the leads and help your ma square away the wagon. I'll finish yoking the oxen. We're on our way."

James knew it was true. They were starting the trek.

# FIVE

## ROLL OUT!

It was already midmorning when Colonel Stewart, on a large white stallion with black spots on his haunches, rode up a small hill overlooking the campsite. James watched as he took off his plumed hat and waved it westward.

"Roll out!" he shouted.

Ma and Elizabeth were sitting in the wagon. Pa walked in front of it, driving the pair of oxen. James walked alongside the wagon. As the lead wagons pulled out of camp, the Walkers came up and waited by the Greggs.

It was a full hour before all twelve wagons were strung out on the trail. The Greggs were midway in the train, for now at least. Leading the train was difficult because sometimes you had to break new trails. But bringing up the rear of the train was worse—you had to breathe in the dust

35

kicked up by everyone else.

Colonel Stewart had established a rotation schedule so that no single wagon got the worst of it at all times. He allowed families to move through the train together if they wished.

Pa controlled the oxen with shouts and by cracking a whip over their heads. James was also good at driving the team. He'd had plenty of practice back home on the farm. He watched his father for a few minutes, then sat down in the dirt, waiting for the Walkers' wagon to come by.

Mr. Walker was having a hard time controlling his six oxen. The Walkers had needed that many to haul all the things they'd brought with them from Philadelphia and purchased in Independence. Mr. Walker wasn't sure how to handle the whip. The team lurched to the right, then to the left. They just weren't obeying his commands.

"This isn't as easy as it looks," he muttered.

"I can show you how to do it," James called from the side of the trail.

"You!" said Mr. Walker.

"He sure can," said Pa. He had dropped back to see why the Walkers were falling behind. "James is good with a team."

James took the whip from Mr. Walker.

"Never hit the oxen," he said. "But give the whip a crack right over their heads. Use your arm and wrist to snap it."

He demonstrated several times, then accompanied the snap with a shout at the oxen. If the oxen veered left, he cracked the whip on that side. If they veered right, he cracked it that way. James shouted at them with each snap. Eventually they'd learn to respond to just the shout. In a few minutes James had the team walking steadily forward, keeping in line.

Then he gave the whip back to Mr. Walker. It didn't take him long to get the knack.

The train moved slowly the first morning. Many of the men had to learn to handle their teams. A number of wagons wandered off the trail. Some teams bolted into others, and several wagons were damaged in collisions.

A cloud of dust thrown up by the hundreds of hooves moved with the train. To keep the dust out of their eyes, many of the emigrants wore handkerchiefs over their faces. The handkerchiefs also helped keep the grit out of their noses and mouths.

By noon the train had gone only two or three miles. That wasn't nearly enough. Colonel Stewart was displeased. He gathered the people together.

"Every hour counts," he said. "Learn how to drive your teams. Do everything as quickly as possible. Help one another. Starting tomorrow, I want the wagons on the trail an hour after sunup."

During "nooning," three riders were sent back to

Independence to fetch forgotten supplies. Since the train hadn't traveled far, they would be able to catch up quickly. It would be the last chance to get supplies for some time. Colonel Stewart said the train should travel fifteen miles a day, especially over the flat prairie, where the trail was usually good.

When the wagons started again, Pa told James he could ride with the Walkers for a while. James, Scott, and Cady sat in the back of the wagon while Mrs. Walker perched up front, reading her Bible. James didn't know how she could do it with all the jouncing.

Then he noticed that the trail dust was bothering Scott. He showed him the best way to tie a handkerchief over his nose and mouth.

"You think you know all the tricks, James," said Cady sarcastically. "You're a regular mountain man."

"I'm just showing you what the men are doing," James said. "Better'n breathing all that dust." He slapped Cady on the back, and she started coughing. "See?"

"Hmph," Cady replied. But James noticed that she took her handkerchief out of her dress pocket and tied it over her face.

James, Scott, and Cady watched several men on horseback ride back and forth among the wagons. They were rounding up livestock that had strayed off the trail. James told Scott that these men didn't have wagons of their own to look after.

"Pa said they're going to Oregon alone," he explained. "They don't have families. So they help as outriders. Or they drive a wagon if someone gets sick or hurt."

Just then a spare ox that Mr. Walker had bought left the line and trotted off the trail, heading for a clump of small trees. Mr. Walker hollered for help, and James watched as an outrider came out of nowhere. He was a young man riding a beautiful jet-black horse with white stockings.

The rider deftly steered his horse behind the ox, driving it in the direction of the Walker wagon. In minutes he had brought the stray back. As the rider approached, James's eyes opened wide. He nudged Scott.

"Isn't that the same fellow who stopped Mackie when he bolted in Independence?" he asked.

Scott squinted. "I reckon it is."

Several of the wagons stopped. The rider dismounted and shook hands with Mr. Walker, who was thanking him heartily.

"Will Gantry," the rider said. "From Culpeper, Virginia. I believe this animal's yours, sir."

By that time James had jumped down off the wagon.

"I saw you in town yesterday," James said. "You were the one who stopped the runaway, weren't you?"

Will peered up at the sky and rubbed his chin. "I do believe I did stop a horse yesterday," he said thoughtfully. Then he smiled and looked down at James. "Though the poor animal was tiring anyway. And who might you be?"

"James Gregg. It was my pa's horse you stopped. His name's Mackie. The horse, I mean." Then he pointed at the Walkers' wagon. "Those're my friends, Scott and Cady Walker. They saw you stop Mackie, too. We thought it was great."

"Well, I'm pleased to meet you, James," Will said. He sat tall in the saddle and held his horse's reins lower down than most of the men. James thought he rode with real style. He had brown eyes and a shock of black hair across his forehead. Will turned to Mr. Walker. "And it was nothing, sir, rounding up that ox. I better get back to out-riding. There'll be plenty of strays the first few days."

James watched Will gallop off. Tomorrow he would ask his pa if he could ride with Will for a while.

Soon afterward a shout went up that riders were coming in. It was the men who had returned to Independence for the supplies.

As the men got closer, James noticed something. On one of the horses there were two riders. James leaped from the Walker wagon and ran to his own.

"Ma, Pa, come quick!" he shouted. "Come quick!"

"What is it, boy?" Pa said. "What's all the ruckus?"

"It's him!" he said, out of breath. "He's riding with one of the other men."

"Who is, son?" Pa asked.

"Jeremy. He's come back."

Pa pulled his team to a halt and quickly helped his wife down from the wagon.

"Are you sure it's him, Jamie?" Ma said.

"Sure I'm sure," said James. "Look."

Ma and Pa squinted through the dust at the hazy figures of the approaching men.

Even Elizabeth was shading her eyes with her hand and gazing into the distance. She hopped from foot to foot with excitement. "Please let it be him, please let it be him," she chanted.

"I don't know . . ." Pa murmured to himself.

Finally they could see for themselves that James was right. It was Jeremy. The man carrying Jeremy on his horse rode by the Gregg wagon, and Jeremy swung off the back.

"Jeremy!" cried Ma.

She raced to her son and threw her arms around him. "My baby!" she said, laughing and crying at the same time. "I was sure I'd never see you again." Then her face went hard, and she pushed him away. "But don't you *ever* do that again!" she hollered, slapping him sharply on the shoulder. Then she grabbed him again and hugged his head.

Jeremy was laughing in spite of himself.

After Ma finally let Jeremy go, Pa put his arm over Jeremy's shoulder and led him to the wagon.

"I'm glad to have you here, son," he said.

"I had to come back," said Jeremy. "I couldn't let you down. My place is with you and Ma until we reach Oregon. Once we're settled there, I can decide what to do."

Then Jeremy looked at James and Elizabeth. "Besides," he said, "I couldn't let my pesky brother and sister have all the fun."

Elizabeth ran over and jumped into Jeremy's arms, and he swung her around. "I'm glad you're back, too!" she shouted.

James wanted to say he had missed him, but he went all shy. "We can always use an extra hand," he said, putting out his own.

Jeremy took it, and they shook like men.

# SIX

## THE THIRD RUNAWAY

What had started as a beautiful spring day was turning gloomy. The wind blew in sudden cold gusts. The blackbirds and crows that James had heard throughout the day were silent. Clouds piled up thickly on the western horizon, and though it was still two hours before sunset, the sky was already as dark as twilight.

Anticipating a storm, Colonel Stewart ordered the wagons to circle for the night in a nearby clearing. The animals were secured by picket lines attached to iron stakes driven into the earth. The emigrants pitched tents inside the circle of wagons.

Jeremy and Pa worked to tie down the animals and find wood for a cook fire while James fetched water from a nearby stream. Ma and Elizabeth were busy clearing ground for the fire. They didn't want to set the prairie ablaze.

43

"Pa!" James called over the wind. "You want me to pitch the tent now?"

"I don't think so, Jamie," he yelled. "I think we'll ride this one out in the wagon."

"But those other folks are pitching theirs," Jeremy argued.

"Those other folks may be sorry they did before the night is over," Pa said. "Now let's help your ma get the fire going."

Soon afterward the Greggs were finishing their dinner of cornmeal cakes fried with strips of fat pork. James thought he'd never tasted anything so delicious, but it might have been because he was so hungry.

No sooner had James licked the last bit of pork fat off his fingers than the storm came. And when it hit, it hit hard. The Greggs ran for the wagon.

Heavy raindrops fell out of the sky in rolling waves, dousing the cook fire in seconds. Loud claps of thunder rattled the wagon and were followed by rumbling echoes that seemed to go on forever. Lightning lit up the prairie with a whitish sparkle brighter than day. In these moments James could see the animals, all standing with their backsides to the wind, heads hung low, eyes shut tight. The darkness that came after the lightning flashes was blacker than midnight.

The wind drove the rain down, then sideways, then upward. Water leaked into the wagon from overhead and blew in through the flaps. Everything was soaked.

James could even feel water coming up through the cracks in the bottom of the wagon. He had never been outside in weather like this before. Back home they had the shelter of their sturdy house. They even had a storm cellar for big blows. On the trail, it was a whole different story.

People were scurrying everywhere. Some were chasing tents that had been picked up by the wind. Others were desperately trying to keep tents from blowing away. James knew Pa had been right about not pitching theirs.

The animals were becoming increasingly nervous at the thunder crashing over them. Horses were straining at their ropes and shaking their heads. James watched as an ox bolted, ripping the stakes that secured its line clean out of the earth and charging away. There was little anyone could do about it at the moment.

Lightning flashed once more, and James saw a young colt come bursting through a sheet of rain. Another flash, and another, and James saw the colt's eyes and nostrils wide with fear at the terrible cracks of thunder. The colt bucked from side to side, kicking out in a frenzy and leaping forward. Then the flashes ended, and the colt was swallowed up by the blackness.

Without a word James sprang from the wagon.

"James!" his pa shouted. "Come back here! You can't stop it."

But James wasn't listening. The colt might hurt itself dashing around blindly like that. He had to do something.

There was another bolt of lightning, and James spotted the colt. It couldn't veer to the left because of the wagons. So James ran at an angle, knowing the colt would have to come right.

James leaped toward the runaway colt, grappling it around the neck just as he had seen Will Gantry do in town the day before. He locked his hands together and held on tight. Then he tried to dig his heels into the wet ground.

"Whoa, boy! Whoa, boy!" he yelled.

James just hung on, shouting, and dug in his heels. He could see the fear in the colt's huge eye and hear its labored breathing. The colt stopped trying to toss James off its neck and began to slow a little. James closed his eyes and buried his face in the colt's wet neck. "Easy, boy, easy," he murmured. "There's a good fella."

Finally the colt came to a stop. It stood trembling with cold and excitement. Still James held on to the colt's neck and talked to the frightened horse for several more minutes.

The storm was breaking as quickly as it had come up. The lightning was less frequent, and the thunder sounded farther and farther away.

At last Pa ran up and slipped a rope around the colt's neck. The animal reared a little once, but James and his pa talked to him and calmed him down.

"That was a mighty foolish thing you did, Jamie," said Pa. "You could have been hurt or killed. But it was very brave. I'm proud of you."

He gave James a pat on the back, and the two of them led the young horse back to the wagon. They tied him between Corncob and Mackie.

"We'll have to find the owner in the morning," Pa said.

They opened the rear flap of the wagon. Ma, Elizabeth, and Jeremy were huddled together under a blanket.

"First Jeremy runs off, now James," said Ma, shaking her head. She turned to Elizabeth. "You better not be planning any tricks, young lady."

"I'm not going *anywhere*," Elizabeth said and snuggled deeper under the blanket.

"And count yourself lucky," Pa told her. "I'm so wet, I better just sit under the wagon. Hand me a blanket and the small stool to sit on. Jamie, since you're so eager to run around in the rain, go and check on the Walkers. Then come right back and join me."

Only a light misty rain was falling now, and when James looked up, he could see the moon beginning to show through the clouds. He trotted over to the Walkers' wagon.

They were safe but very wet. Scott wasn't breathing well, and he looked terrible. With her hair plastered down around her neck and shoulders, Cady looked even more rawboned than usual. James didn't tell them about saving the colt. That could wait until morning.

James went back to his family's wagon and sat under it with his pa. The night had turned cold fast. James couldn't stop shivering. When he saw that his pa was shivering too, he decided not to complain.

A few people managed to get small fires going. They were smoky because the wood was wet. A larger fire was finally lit in the middle of the circled wagons. The bigger it got, the faster it dried the wet wood, and the cleaner it burned. The Greggs, along with the Walkers and almost everyone else on the train, gathered around it.

"We'll get a lot of storms on the prairie," Colonel Stewart told the emigrants. "You won't be able to build a bonfire every time. There might not be enough wood. Better learn how to handle the storms—secure everything and keep your things dry."

"I knew I was a fool to come back," Jeremy muttered, his voice still quivering with the cold. "If this is how the rest of the trip is gonna be . . . well, I should have gone home."

"Pa meant what he said," James told his brother. "We need you here where you belong."

Jeremy looked down at his little brother. "No sense talking about it anymore. I'm here and that's that. But I'm not cut out for this kind of life."

"Pa will teach us," said James. Jeremy shrugged and walked away.

James looked at the faces around the fire. Not too many looked happy. He heard Scott try to stifle a cough, then give in to it. Suddenly James felt more tired than he had ever been. He thought about his warm, dry bed back on the farm. Then he felt a hand on his shoulder.

"Hey, James, you all right? You look like a wet hen."

James turned to see Will Gantry standing beside him. Will was just as soaked as he was, but was managing a smile.

James told him about the colt he had stopped. "Do you know who owns him?"

"He might belong to the Meachams, by the way you describe him," Will said. "Tell you what. I'll come by in the morning and we'll find out for sure. You better get some sleep now. Colonel Stewart wants us rolling by seven."

# SEVEN

## BOLT

Will was right. Before dawn the sharp report of a night sentry's rifle jerked James from a restless sleep.

It was hard to set the morning fires because everything was still soaked. Some of the men were out searching for animals that had run off during the storm. But when the griddle cakes with molasses and bacon were finally dished out, they tasted finer than anything.

Just before the wagons were to line up, Will came by. He had been with the men looking for the missing livestock. He and James went over to the colt and untied it.

"Not much of an animal, is it?" James said, looking the bony colt up and down. He could see the lines of its ribs showing through its dull dun coat. It was a bit knock-kneed, and its withers stuck out in a sharp knob. When James passed his hand over its flank, the colt trembled nervously even though the terrors of the night before had long since passed.

"I have seen finer horses in my time," Will said judiciously.

"I like him anyway," James decided aloud, looking the colt in the eye. The colt glared at James with a mixture of fear, defiance, and curiosity. "He has spirit."

"That's as may be," said Will, "but there's nothing for it now but to take him back to his owner."

"Right," said James. "Lead the way."

They walked across camp to the Meacham wagon.

Mr. Meacham did own the colt. He was a tall, skinny man with a wispy graying beard. When Will told him what had happened, Meacham shook his head in disgust.

"Can't say I'm glad to see him back," Meacham muttered. "He's been sickly since the day he was foaled. I never thought he'd last the winter, let alone two. Just look at him." He took a step toward the colt, and the scrawny animal backed away, snorting sharply. James patted the colt's neck to quiet him.

"I've got enough stock to worry about as it is," Meacham went on. "I oughta just put him down and sell his hide to the Indians."

"Put him down?" said James, shocked. He exchanged looks with Will.

"He eats good oats, don't he?" Meacham said bitterly. "Better I waste a bullet than any more feed on that worthless bag of bones."

"No need to do that, now, Mr. Meacham," said Will. "This boy will take good care of him. Won't you, James?"

"What? Oh, uh, yeah," James answered, startled. "I sure will, Mr. Meacham."

"Take him," said Meacham. "He's yours. And good riddance to him."

"You mean it?" said James. He couldn't believe anyone would actually give him a horse, even if the horse was just a worthless bag of bones. "You'll give him to me?"

"Kid, I'd rather see him eat your oats than mine." Meacham spat a bright red stream of tobacco juice. "He's never gonna amount to nothing anyways." He turned and headed back for his wagon.

Will started to lead James and the colt away. "Let's get out of here while the gettin's good," he whispered.

But James called out, "Mr. Meacham."

"Yeah?" the man replied, pivoting.

"What's his name?"

"Whose name?"

"The colt's."

"The colt's?" Meacham gave a short, barking

laugh. "That colt don't have a name. Didn't give him one. Like I said, never thought he'd last the winter." Meacham walked away, shaking his head and chuckling.

"Yeah, well," James muttered to himself, "he did last the winter, didn't he?" Then he turned to Will. "Thanks for helping me with Mr. Meacham."

"No true-blue Virginian forsakes a good horse," said Will loftily.

"I can't believe I have my very own colt," James murmured. "Now I just have to make Pa understand."

Will eyed the bony colt. "Good luck with that."

"Thanks," said James. "I'll need it."

Pa took some convincing. He knew the colt wasn't much to look at. But he also knew how much the colt already meant to James. And he couldn't help liking him himself.

"That colt does have spirit, Jamie," he said, running his hand down the animal's spine. "Though he is rather lean."

"He's skinny!" Elizabeth laughed. She was dancing around the colt excitedly.

"Lean! Skinny!" snorted Jeremy. "Why, that colt doesn't have an ounce of meat on him."

"He will," said James. "I'm sure Mr. Meacham wasn't caring for him properly. I can fatten him up. You'll see. Can I keep him, Pa?"

"We don't have a lot of feed to spare, son. . . ." Pa saw the disappointment rising in James and Elizabeth's faces. "But then again, it doesn't look like he eats much."

James broke into a smile.

"You know you'll have to take care of the colt and still do all your regular chores," Pa added.

"I know that, sir," James agreed quickly.

"What're you gonna call him, Jamie?" Elizabeth piped up.

There was a moment of silence while James looked thoughtfully at the sky. "I was thinking I'd call him Bolt," he said. "'Cause the first time I saw him, it was in a bolt of lightning."

"Bolt's a fine name for that colt," Jeremy teased. "Mighty fine. 'Cause he's so skittish, he's always trying to *bolt*." He laughed loudly.

Pa shot Jeremy a stern look. "I think it's a fine name, Jamie. Bolt. It suits him."

Not all the livestock had been recovered by the time Colonel Stewart gave the signal for the train to break circle and form a line. Many of the emigrants were upset. James was yoking the oxen when he heard some men yelling.

"It was Indians. I know it was Indians," one of the outriders was saying. "Them savages is just waiting for a chance to steal our horses."

"Calm down, Mr. Carver," said Colonel Stewart, who had also heard the commotion. "Animals panic in a storm. They can easily get lost. And besides, it's oxen, not horses, that are missing."

"Maybe," said Carver. "But if I see an Indian around my animals, I'll shoot him. I swear I will."

"You'll keep your finger off the trigger if you know what's good for you, Carver," said Colonel Stewart. "Shoot anyone and you put us all at risk."

Carver grunted and went back to work. The colonel rode off at a brisk canter to check on the other wagons.

Later James told his pa what he had heard, and asked if Indians could have stolen the animals.

"It's possible," said Pa. "I heard Indians will steal sometimes, but I don't really know. You hear lots of things. What we don't need, though, is a hothead like Jenson Carver."

Because of rumors about Indians, the emigrants had come heavily armed. As James had noticed, guns were a big part of P. Whitfield's business back in Independence. All the men carried pistols, and many of the women did too. Every family had at least one black-powder single-shot rifle. Some had two or three rifles always loaded, cocked, and ready to fire. Yet many of these same people had little or no experience with firearms.

The wagons rolled on. Later that day a cheer went up when Colonel Stewart announced they had just left Missouri and crossed into the Unorganized Territory.

It was the first time James had ever been outside the twenty-nine states. The twenty-nine states. It had a funny ring to it. When James was little, there had been only twenty-six. But in 1845, when he was eight, Florida had entered the Union. Later in that same year, Texas joined up. Texas! James marveled at the idea of it. Texas used to be its own country, and now it was just another state. The year after that, Iowa became a state. Now they were saying Wisconsin was going to be next.

James looked around him at the empty prairie.

"Hey, Pa," he called out. "You reckon this land'll ever get to be a state?"

"I suppose one day it might," Pa said.

"How 'bout Oregon Territory, and all the country in between?"

"There's mighty big country out West, son," said Pa. "I don't know if there'll ever be enough people to make states out of it. Maybe in a couple hundred years. In the meantime, the Indians are welcome to it."

James liked the thought of there being enough land for everybody.

# EIGHT

## TRAPPING A GOPHER

"Got you, Jamie!" Scott said, laughing. "Now you're It."

James shut his eyes and commenced counting. "Ten, twenty, thirty . . ."

Scott ducked into a dry creekbed while Cady crouched behind some scrub brush.

"One hundred!" James hollered. "Here I come!"

He ran across the flat, sun-baked prairie. Above him the blue, cloudless sky arched down to meet green grass that stretched off to the horizon.

It seemed like a silent land, but when James stopped to listen for Scott or Cady's giggling, he realized how alive the prairie was with sound. Grasshoppers trilled, crows cawed, and meadowlarks burst into showers of song. Even the grass was noisy as it rustled in the breeze.

James, Scott, and Cady had finished their suppers

59

of roast rabbit and corn cakes. Despite the morning's tiring walk, even Scott was full of energy. While the grown-ups rested for the afternoon's trek, the three of them played in the prairie. But they were not supposed to stray far from the wagons.

James spotted a patch of blue gingham showing through the branches of a nearby bush.

"I see you, Cady!" he shouted, trotting toward the bush.

Cady screamed, laughing, and took off running.

James sprinted after her, leaping over the tufts of high grass and dodging around scrub. He tagged her shoulder and they both fell over giggling. Scott flopped down beside them on the dusty ground. He picked up a stick and poked it into an anthill.

"Look at those fellas go," Scott said, pointing to the little black ants. They were swarming around the stick, which was blocking the hole to their nest.

James reached over and rattled the stick around, scattering dirt and ants. "Cyclone!" he shouted. "Run for cover, boys!"

Cady snatched the stick out of his hand. "That's not funny, James," she said. "Why're you being so mean?"

"They're just *ants*, Cady," Scott said.

"Yeah," said James. Who cared about a bunch of little ants? Still, he didn't like to see Cady disapprove of him.

"You shouldn't ruin their home," Cady said, toss-

60

ing the stick away. "Even if they are just ants." She got up, clapping the dust off her hands. "Let's go exploring."

"All right," said James. He was glad Cady had decided to change the subject.

There were interesting things to discover all around them. The prairie was hopping with jackrabbits. The first time he'd seen one, James had been surprised by how big and lean it was. It was nothing like the plump little balls of fur they had for rabbits on the farm back home. Jackrabbits seemed all long, skinny ears and long, scrawny legs. But they made good eating, that was for sure.

In the late afternoons, after they'd made camp, James's Pa went out hunting, and almost every day he'd bring back something. In addition to jackrabbits, the prairie was full of antelopes, deer, pheasants, partridges, prairie hens, and squirrels. The creeks and ponds were stocked with fish and ducks. Pa said they should live off the land while they could, because soon enough they'd be entering country where the game was less plentiful.

But the animal that outnumbered all the rest of them put together was the gopher. Even the jackrabbits seemed scarce in comparison.

Gophers were little brown-striped critters. To James they looked like the chipmunks that lived in the woodpile back home in Pennsylvania. But gophers lived in holes in the ground like ants.

And those holes were everywhere.

James knew he had to watch where he stepped when he ran across the prairie—put your foot in a gopher hole, and you could break an ankle easy! Mr. Loughery had had to put down one of his horses after it had snapped a leg in a gopher hole.

James, Scott, and Cady watched the gophers pop in and out of their holes. Suddenly a hawk that had been circling overhead fell out of the sky. The gopher it was aiming for dived into its hole, and the hawk flapped away. After a few seconds the gopher reappeared at a nearby hole, chattering loudly and kicking up dirt.

"Did you see how he got away from that hawk?" Cady said. "Those holes must be connected by tunnels."

"I wonder if they're all linked up," James said. He scanned the prairie. Gophers were popping in and out of holes as far as the eye could see.

"I bet that gopher could make it all the way to Oregon underground," Scott said, pointing to the one that had escaped the hawk.

"Maybe so," said Cady. "But he'd have pretty sore paws by the time he got there."

"At least he wouldn't have to worry about hawks if he stayed underground," said Scott. "Say, James. D'you suppose we could catch us a gopher?"

"They're quicker than we are," said James. "Even quicker than hawks." Then he smiled slyly. "But we're smarter. Let's run back to the wagons for a minute. I need to get some things."

Ten minutes later all three were lying in the hot prairie dust behind a line of scrub, trying not to laugh. James held a string. About fifteen feet away, the other end of the string was tied to a short stick. The stick propped up an upside-down empty bushel basket, which James had borrowed from his ma.

A gopher was nosing around the stick.

"C'mon, fella," James murmured. "Just a couple more inches."

James had placed a few grains of feed corn underneath the basket as bait. The gopher spotted the corn and took a tentative step toward it.

"C'mon . . ." Scott whispered.

The gopher scampered under the basket. It started scooping up the grains with its front paws and tucking them in its cheeks.

James gave the string a sharp yank, the stick went flying, and the basket dropped over the gopher.

"Got 'im!" Scott hollered, leaping up.

The three dashed over to the basket. They could hear the gopher scrabbling at the inside, trying to get out.

"What do we do with him now?" Cady asked.

"Kill him, I reckon," said James.

"Kill him?"

"Why, sure," James replied. "There's not much meat on a gopher, but he'll make a fine stew for breakfast tomorrrow."

"I wouldn't have helped you if I'd known you were planning on killing him," said Cady.

"What did you think we were gonna do?" Scott asked. "Saddle him up and ride off on him? He's just a gopher."

"Besides," said James, "you weren't much help anyway. All you did was giggle."

Cady whacked James hard on the shoulder. "James Gregg!" she said. "I'm ashamed of you. You know we don't need that gopher. Your pa gets us plenty of rabbit and deer to eat. You just want to kill him for the fun of it!"

She stalked off, kicking up dust in front of her.

"What a baby." Scott laughed. "Now let's get your pa's gun and finish the job."

"She's right, you know," said James. He could hear the gopher chattering excitedly underneath the basket. "Maybe we shouldn't kill the poor critter. We don't need the meat."

Scott was silent for a moment. "Whatever you say," he muttered and kicked over the basket. The gopher shot away and dived down a nearby hole. "I hope you're happy now."

"Aw, Scott . . ." James started, but Scott had already turned back for the wagons.

Now both of his friends were mad at him—Cady

for his wanting to kill the gopher, and Scott for his not wanting to. James kicked at the ground and headed deeper into the prairie.

He came upon the dry creekbed Cady had been hiding in earlier and followed it a ways. Most of the prairie was covered with grass and scrub, but trees grew in the creekbeds. Their gnarled roots snaked around rocks and plunged into the earth, sucking at the water that collected there. He stepped in rhythm with the buzzing of the insects that lived among the roots.

James was about to round a bend in the creekbed when he heard voices above the insects' trilling. His first thought was *Indians*! A shiver of fear ran down his spine. He stood stock-still and listened closely. It sounded like the Indians were giggling. That was odd.

Then he heard one of them say, "You're prettier than a rosebud on a June morning, Miss Sara."

James sighed in relief and stepped around the bend. "Boy, did you give me a fri—"

"Jamie! What are you doing here?" It was Will Gantry. He was sitting with a young woman in a shady nook of the creek bank. In one hand he held a bunch of wildflowers. His other hand was wrapped around the young woman's waist.

"I—I—" James stammered.

The young woman hopped to her feet and commenced brushing her hair back and smoothing down her dress. "I believe it's time we got back to the wagons, Mr. Gantry," she said stiffly. "Nooning will be about over."

"Certainly," Will said. He got up. "Er, Jamie, this is Miss Sara Jennington. Sara, James Gregg." He clapped his hands nervously. "Well, we best get back."

"Thank you for showing me those very fascinating rock formations, Mr. Gantry," Sara said with an exaggerated formality. "I do so enjoy speaking with someone who shares my interest in geology."

"We must do it again someday, Miss Jennington," said Will.

James stifled a laugh.

"Quite," said Sara.

By now James had had a chance to take a good look at her. Her shiny black hair fell in loose curls onto her shoulders. She had a small nose and chin, and large velvet brown eyes set off by long black lashes. James wasn't sure if her cheeks always had that healthy flush, or if she was just blushing with embarrassment. Either way, James decided Will was right—she was prettier than a rosebud on a June morning.

"What're you gawking at, boy?" Will suddenly said to James. "Let's get going." He handed Sara out of the creekbed, then helped James up too. As James was walking away, Will reached over and twisted his ear playfully—but hard enough to let James know he was mad at him.

*Join the crowd*, James thought morosely.

# NINE

## KAWS AND POTAWATOMI

S oon the train turned northward. It was heading for Nebraska Territory and the Platte River, which the emigrants would follow to Fort Laramie. Fort Laramie was the first place they would be able to stop for a real rest and buy supplies. It would take more than six weeks to get there.

James spent much of his time driving the team, riding Corncob, and caring for Bolt. Meacham had never bothered to break Bolt, even though he was more than two years old. He was so sickly, he couldn't be ridden anyway. James was determined to nurse the colt to health and ride him before they got to Oregon.

The train reached the south bank of the Wakarusa River. It was the first large river they'd had to cross. The Wakarusa was shallow enough to ford—the draft animals would simply pull the wagons across.

It was a risky method of traversing a river. The currents were often hard to judge, and animals, whole wagons, even people had been known to be swept away during fordings. But it was a lot quicker than building rafts and floating everything over.

While Colonel Stewart organized the wagons for the fording, James untied Bolt and walked him downriver a ways. Cady and Scott soon joined him.

"Can I walk him?" Scott asked. It was the first time he'd spoken to James since they'd let the gopher go.

"Sure," said James, handing him the rope. "Go slowly."

"I'm not mad at you anymore," said Scott, walking Bolt in a small circle. "I reckon Cady was right about the gopher."

"I'm not mad at you either," said Cady. "Seeing as how I was right all along."

James grinned. "I'm glad for that. I needed someone to help me with Bolt."

The colt pawed the ground, threw his head back and forth, then playfully nudged Scott in the back, causing him to stumble slightly.

Cady laughed. "I think he likes you."

"I can't wait to ride him. You'll let me, won't you, James?" said Scott.

"First let's get you used to riding Corncob," James replied. "She's a sweet old nag and won't give you any trouble."

Just then Will came riding up on his big black stallion. He dismounted and slapped Bolt on the shoulder. Bolt shook his mane and whinnied. He was prancing with energy, not fear.

"Looks better already, James," Will said consideringly. He hadn't mentioned the incident with Sara Jennington to James since it had happened. "Take good care of him, and you'll have a fine horse before you know it."

James beamed. Will had grown up on a plantation in Virginia and knew horses. He was a good judge of horseflesh.

"You think it'll be easy crossing this river, Will?" James asked.

"All rivers can be dangerous, I reckon," Will said. "But we won't have any trouble with the Wakarusa."

"That's good," Cady said, "because I can't swim a lick."

James was always surprised to learn what Scott and Cady couldn't do. They didn't know how to ride. They couldn't swim. Neither one of them had ever shot a gun. James wondered what city kids did all day. Read books, he guessed.

"Look, everybody!" Scott whispered nervously. "Indians."

All heads turned. Coming down the bluff on the opposite bank were six Indians—four young men who looked to be about Will's age, and two older men. Some carried bows and arrows, while others had long lances. They were bare chested and wore deerskin trousers, plus short cloths around their waists and hips. Their heads were bare except for a tuft of hair running along the top and down the back.

"Look at them," Cady murmured.

"Should we run back to the wagons?" James whispered to Will.

"No," he said softly. "They're Kansa Indians. Some folks call 'em Kaws. No need for us to worry. I hear they're peaceful—probably just here to trade. As long as we stick by the train, we have nothing to fear from them."

James and the others headed back upriver slowly, so as not to alarm the Indians.

The Kaws, however, stayed where they were and watched the wagons prepare to ford. By now there was a great deal of talk among the emigrants. James could see rifles appearing at many of the wagons, and lots of men were fingering their pistols nervously.

Finally Colonel Stewart approached the Kaws. He wasn't armed. James could see him greet them, but he couldn't hear what was being said.

"I don't trust 'em hangin' around," James heard someone say angrily. It was Jenson Carver, the man who had talked about shooting Indians before. He was waving a pistol. "I say we run 'em off."

"And you will say no more, Mr. Carver," said Pierre Delaroux. "They will not attack us. We are many, and those Kaws, they are few. They are here to trade. We must guard ourselves, that is true. But we should not look for trouble, or trouble will find us." He grinned threateningly at Carver. "Or trouble will find *you*, Mr. Carver."

James heard several men mutter in agreement with Delaroux. But Carver was still waving his pistol.

"Now I suggest, Mr. Carver," said Delaroux, "that you put your gun away, before someone"—he looked Carver in the eye and said the word again—"someone gets hurt."

Carver saw that he had no support among the other men and holstered his pistol. He went back to his wagon, muttering to himself.

"I've seen Jenson Carver's kind before," Will said to James. "There was an overseer like him back home. A cruel man and a bully. He won't be happy till he starts something with the Indians."

James breathed a big sigh of relief when he felt his wagon's front wheels bump onto the north bank of the Wakarusa. The rest of the train also forded the river without incident. The Kaws accompanied the train for a few more miles, then went away peacefully. It occurred to James that the Indians were simply seeing them out of their territory.

* * *

The land was mostly flat as they headed north-west for the Platte. Twice more James spotted a few Kaw Indians watching the train, even following it for a few miles. Guards were doubled, but as Delaroux had promised, nothing happened.

The emigrants forded the Kansas, a broad, shallow river, and the Vermillion. They began seeing a different kind of Indian. Delaroux said they were Potawatomi.

One day, as the wagons were circling up for camp, a number of Potawatomi came walking slowly toward them. They were tall and wiry, and carried themselves with a proud formality. James thought many of the young men were quite handsome, and the women very beautiful. The Potawatomi had long, straight, flowing black hair and colorful clothing adorned by strands of beads.

Once again the guns were ready, but the Potawatomi had come unarmed. They offered dried buffalo meat and cornmeal, as well as blankets, beads, and deerskin leggings.

Colonel Stewart told the emigrants they could trade with the Indians if they wanted to. Many of them gathered items from their wagons.

James's ma got out a little pillow embroidered with daisies, and one of Pa's old calico work shirts. Pa fetched a corncob pipe and some tobacco.

"Ask your ma and pa if you can come with us to meet the Indians," James said to Scott and Cady. The

Walkers were not going to be trading anything. Mrs. Walker didn't want to have anything to do with Indians.

Scott and Cady ran to ask their parents. Then James heard Mrs. Walker cry, "Absolutely not! You will stay here with me in the wagon until those heathens go away."

"But Mother, the Greggs are going to trade," Scott said. "Can't we just go with them?"

"Please, Mother," Cady begged.

"Why don't we let the children go, Rebecca," Mr. Walker said soothingly. "These Indians seem harmless enough. And I'm sure Amelia will watch the children carefully."

"But John . . ." Mrs. Walker started. Then she pursed her lips and pulled her shawl around her tighter.

"Go on now, children," Mr. Walker said.

As Scott and Cady skipped over to James, he saw Mr. Walker put his arm around his wife. She shuddered and drew away.

The two groups gathered to trade in a clearing near the wagons. The Potawatomi carefully examined all the things the emigrants were offering. They were especially fascinated by a mirror. They took turns peering into it and gasping in surprise at their own reflections. James and Cady laughed when they saw that.

The Potawatomi didn't speak English, so all the

bartering was done with gestures. Several times they spoke quietly to one another. James watched them closely. He wasn't frightened at all. They didn't look fierce or savage. He thought they were cleaner and better dressed than most of the people on the wagon train.

Several Indians looked over the goods James's folks had brought.

A man about Pa's age picked up the corncob pipe and sucked on it. He seemed pleased but uncertain. When he went to place it back down, Pa took his hands and folded them around the pipe. Then Pa offered him the small sack of tobacco. The man understood, and accepted the items.

A young man and woman came up. They were holding hands. They reminded James of Will and Sara Jennington. The young man chose Pa's blue work shirt.

"You'll look handsome in that," Ma said, smiling. Even though the man could not have known what she was saying, James judged from his face that he had understood the compliment. Then the young girl at his side pointed shyly to the pillow Ma had brought.

"I think she likes it," Pa said. Ma handed her the pillow. The young woman broke into a wide grin, giggled, and then hid her face behind the man's shoulder.

Just then Jeremy came riding up on Mackie. An

old man walked over to them and commenced looking Mackie over. He checked his teeth and felt along his chest and legs. Then he stepped back and motioned at Mackie and Jeremy. Pa shook his head.

"No," he said. "Not the horse. I can't trade that."

"Maybe he wants Jeremy," James joked. Cady and Scott guffawed loudly.

Jeremy dismounted. "I'd gladly give *you* to him," he said to James. "And throw in a sack of flour for his trouble."

"Hush, Jeremy," Pa said. "That goes for both of you."

Again the old man motioned at Mackie. This time he said some words in a language James didn't understand.

"No," Pa repeated, gesturing with his hands. He told Jeremy to take Mackie away, which he did quickly.

The Potawatomi talked among themselves. Then they displayed the things they had brought. Ma selected a warm-looking blanket and a strand of beads from the young man and woman who had acquired the shirt and pillow.

The man who was now lighting up the corncob pipe offered Pa his own long-stemmed pipe, called a calumet, in exchange for it. Pa gladly accepted the bargain.

"I believe I'll smoke a peace pipe with this fellow," Pa said as the Indian pinched some tobacco in his new pipe.

James, Cady, and Scott watched the men tamp down the bowls and light up. "Ask him!" Cady whispered, elbowing James sharply in the ribs. Scott snickered nervously.

"Er, Pa? Can we have a smoke too?" James asked.

"I don't know about your friends, but you may."

James's jaw dropped. "You mean it?"

His pa nodded. "When you're older, boy," he said, puffing contentedly. "When you're older."

James watched enviously as his pa traded pipes back and forth with the man. Back East the papers called Indians dirty, wild, and cruel, but this man seemed as well mannered as his own father. He wondered what other new things he would learn on the way to Oregon.

# TEN

## THE LIVING SEA

As the wagons moved farther up the Little Blue and closer to the Platte, the country changed. The land was flatter and drier. They were entering Pawnee Indian country now. The Pawnee were rumored to be more hostile to emigrants than their neighbors to the east.

There were no more lush green valleys between the stretches of grassy prairie. It was becoming more difficult to find wood for the fires. Finally there simply wasn't enough.

"What are we going to do?" James asked his folks. "If we can't find firewood, how will we stay warm at night? And Ma won't be able to bake bread."

Pa took a deep breath. "I don't know," he said. "Just a few days ago there was more wood than we could use. I'm sure Colonel Stewart knew this would happen. I'll have to find out."

A short time later Pierre Delaroux rode past. Pa stopped him and asked about the lack of firewood. Delaroux gave a huge belly laugh.

"I'm glad you're laughing, Mr. Delaroux," Pa said, "but I can't say as I see what's so funny."

"Ah, we have all the fuel we need," Delaroux answered, wiping his eyes. "And more. We are in the land of the buffaloes."

Delaroux galloped a distance from the wagon, jumped off his horse, and picked something up. Then he rode back.

"You may thank the buffaloes," he said, chuckling. He held out what looked like a piece of rotted wood. "This is what you burn now."

Pa squinted up at Delaroux. "Well, I'll be . . ." Then he and Ma started laughing.

"It's not manna from heaven," she said, "but it'll do."

For a moment James didn't get it. Then he looked again at what Delaroux was holding. He realized it was a buffalo chip. A piece of dried dropping. Dung.

"Well, I'll be . . ." he said like his pa had.

James soon learned that the chips burned like coal, giving off more than enough heat for cooking. They didn't burn very cleanly—there was always plenty of smoke. But the smoke had a sweet odor that wasn't at all unpleasant.

One day James asked Will, "Why haven't we seen any buffalo yet? Their chips are all over the place."

"Eager for a hunt?" Will teased.

"And why not?" James shot back. "I can handle a gun. You should've seen me picking off squirrels back home."

"I don't doubt it," Will said seriously. "But buffalo are a little bigger than squirrels. They can trample a man dead and not even notice it."

"You're not scared, are you?" James asked. It never occurred to him that Will might be afraid of something.

Will shook his head. "Not scared, no. But between you and me, the biggest animal I ever shot was a pig for slaughter. When the buffalo come around, I'll be ready for 'em. But I'm no fool. I won't be taking any chances."

James remembered the way Will had risked his life to stop Mackie back in Independence. If he talked about buffalo this way, they must be dangerous.

James knew immediately that the roar wasn't thunder. But if it wasn't a storm, what could it be? His heart pounding in his chest, he raised his head and saw a faint orange light coming in through the flaps of the tent. It was almost sunup.

The roar grew louder. James could feel the ground shaking. Now Jeremy was sitting up beside him in the tent. He looked bewildered and a little frightened.

"What in the world is that?" he whispered.

"I don't know," James said.

Just then someone yelled the word that all emigrants on the plains feared: *"Stampede!"*

James bolted from the tent, Jeremy right behind him. There were people scurrying everywhere. Dust sifted into the rosy light of dawn, making it hard to see very far. Men were shouting orders and gathering their families, and little children were screaming in their mothers' arms.

"Ma! Pa!" James yelled. He checked the tent where they had been sleeping with Elizabeth. They were gone.

James ran to the wagon and grabbed his rifle, then headed in the direction of the thundering. Other men were going that way too, James noticed, and they were all carrying guns.

Because they feared the Pawnee, the emigrants had pitched their tents inside the circle of wagons. James squirmed his way through the crowd of men till he reached the wagons on the western side of the circle.

Beyond them, about two hundred yards away, he saw a herd of buffalo twenty or so deep streaming southward over a rise. James had never before seen animals so big galloping so fast. They didn't look much bigger than his pa's oxen, but they were much quicker. They held their huge heads low to the ground as they ran, so low that their long, goatlike beards nearly trailed in the dirt. Their great shoulders matted with thick brown wool pumped and strained as they pounded the earth. The sun glinted off their small, sharp horns.

James had seen drawings in newspapers of buffalo. Somehow he'd pictured them as looking like Bruno, Mr. Holtzbrink's fat, lazy bull back home. But these buffalo were much hairier than Bruno. And more muscular. And meaner looking.

"How can they make so much noise?" James shouted to Pierre Delaroux, who was standing beside him. "There aren't *that* many of them."

"Aren't that many of them!" Delaroux repeated. He let out a loud, hooting laugh. "My friend, peek over that ridge, please, and you will see more buffaloes than you ever imagined!"

"Delaroux's right!" Pa shouted. He had just made it to the front. "Colonel Stewart says this herd may go on for miles. He was just telling the men what to do if the herd turned toward us."

"What's that?" James asked.

"Start firing, hope for the best, and make your peace."

James turned back to the herd with renewed respect, and not a little fear. The roaring, thundering sound merged with the trembling of the earth under his feet. The flow of animals from right to left

81

over the rise was mesmerizing.

Suddenly some of the animals broke away from the main stream. They were coming for the camp. There were only a couple of dozen of them, but if more buffalo followed, they could flatten every man, woman, and child in the train.

Colonel Stewart left the circle of wagons and rode straight for the onrushing buffalo. Then he swung around on his horse. *"Every man with a gun line up here!"* he hollered. *"Fire into the air to divert them! Shoot the leaders if you have to!"*

James lunged forward, but his pa held him back.

"No, James," he said. "I need you to take care of your ma and Elizabeth."

"But, Pa—"

"Do as I say, boy." He squeezed James's shoulder and took off between the wagons to join the other men. Some were already firing their guns into the air. The breakaway herd kept coming and was now less than a hundred yards from the train.

*"Form two lines!"* Colonel Stewart shouted, waving a saber in the air. *"Load your weapons and aim for the leaders!"*

The men in front dropped to one knee. James saw that Will was among them. The men in the second line stood. Pa was standing, the last man on the left side.

*"Fire!"* the colonel screamed.

The guns sounded at once. A line of smoke rose,

was caught by the breeze, and scattered. Several of the lead buffalo stumbled for a stride or two, but only one of them fell. James could see spots of red on the ones that had stumbled.

Some of the men had brought more than one rifle. They quickly fired them. Again only one buffalo fell.

"*Reload!*"

The buffalo kept coming. James stood behind the wagons and prayed, his heart in his throat.

"*Fire!*"

This time the two lead buffalo, which had already been wounded, dropped and rolled. The ones behind them dodged the fallen bodies and kept coming. The buffalo would be on top of the men before they could reload and get off another volley.

The men in the lines tried to scramble away, but there were too many of them. They were getting in each other's way. James saw that the men on the end of the line were going to be trampled.

"Pa!" he shouted. "Look out!"

At the last instant, when the buffalo were only twenty yards from the men, they veered as one to the left, back toward the main herd.

But James could see that there were too many buffalo in the breakaway herd to make the sharp turn away from the line of men. And Pa was the closest to the onrushing animals. The men to his right were falling over each other in their attempt to flee. Pa wouldn't be able to make it.

"*Pa!*" James screamed.

A buffalo was bearing down on his pa. Blood was spraying from wounds on its woolly brown shoulder and on its muzzle. James knew nothing could stop it, and that his pa was going to be trampled.

Suddenly someone grabbed the rifle out of James's hands and vaulted between the wagons. It was Jeremy! James watched in astonishment as Jeremy raised the rifle to his shoulder and aimed for the buffalo coming at Pa. James prayed that his brother would get off the shot of his life.

*Crack!* Jeremy fired. There was a burst of red right between the huge brown eyes of the buffalo, and it pitched forward over its front legs. It tumbled straight for Pa, who was still trying desperately to scramble away. Over and over the great beast rolled, two times, three, until it crashed into Pa, slamming him to the ground. When the tremendous beast finally came to a rest, Pa's legs were pinned beneath its hindquarters.

The remaining buffalo had turned sharply to the left, away from the men. James and Jeremy rushed up and helped Will and some other men drag Pa out from under the fallen buffalo. They carried him back to the wagons.

"Pa!" James shouted. "Pa!" He was sure his father was dead.

They laid Pa down inside the circle of wagons.

The buffalo were still thundering past, but James no longer heard them.

"Pa! Don't die!"

"Stop your hollering, boy," said Pa groggily. "I'm not dead yet."

James laughed. He laughed so hard that tears came streaming down his cheeks. He was sure they hadn't been there before.

"I'm not dead yet," Pa repeated, "thanks to you, Jeremy." He grasped his older son's arm, groaning with the effort. "That was quite a shot. You saved your old pa's life."

"Easy there," Jeremy said, gently placing Pa's hand on his chest. "You're all bruised up."

"But not dead." Pa smiled and closed his eyes. "Not dead." He opened them again. "Now, aren't you glad you came?"

"I reckon I am, sir," Jeremy said with a grin. "I reckon I am."

James knew that what Pa had said was true. Jeremy had saved their pa's life. His brother was a hero.

It was more than two hours before the last buffalo galloped by. The afternoon was spent butchering the five that had been killed. There were hundreds of pounds of meat to be divided up, and the hides would make fine blankets and robes.

Although the stampede had caused the train to

lose a day, no one complained. The meat they acquired made the delay worthwhile.

Pa was sore but had no broken bones. Jeremy and James volunteered to take turns driving the oxen for the next few days while Pa rode in the wagon.

That afternoon James, Scott, and Cady followed Will and Jeremy up to the rise and looked out over the valley below.

"Look at 'em all," Will said. "There must be a million of 'em."

To the south and west was a great brown mass of buffalo stretching off to the horizon. Though the bulk of the herd was now miles away, James could feel the ground trembling a little with their pounding.

"A sea of buffalo," James murmured. He had never seen the ocean, but he knew it could not possibly be more thrilling than this. "A living sea."

Jeremy nodded. "There's enough meat in that herd alone to feed the whole country for a thousand years."

"That's the truth," said Will. "That's surely the truth."

The five stood on the rise and quietly watched the vast herd make its way toward the horizon.

## Eleven

## The Silent Ones

Days ran into each other. The land was flat and featureless, and the blue sky was rarely broken by a cloud. The wind kicked up the dust and made breathing difficult, staying clean impossible.

James was glad when his pa was strong enough to drive the oxen again. What with his regular chores, caring for Bolt, and driving the team, he had had no time left over for himself. He hadn't seen much of Cady or Scott for several days and was eager to find out how they were doing.

"Howdy, Scott, Cady!" he hollered, trotting up on Corncob. The train had stopped for the evening, but sunset was still a couple of hours away.

"Howdy, James!" they yelled, hopping off the back of their wagon.

"What d'you say I give you that riding lesson you've been waiting for?"

87

"I'd love it," Cady said.

"Me too," Scott added. "I've been looking forward to—"

"I'm not sure that's such a good idea, James," came a voice from inside the wagon. Mrs. Walker's face appeared at the back flap. "Horses are awfully dangerous, aren't they?"

"Who, Corncob?" James asked. He patted her neck. "She's the gentlest thing on four hooves. Wouldn't hurt a fly."

"Still, I . . ."

"Don't you fret, ma'am," said James. "I've been riding since I was five, and never been hurt yet. I'll be careful with Cady and Scott."

"I don't know . . ."

"Please, Mother?" said Scott. "Now that we're out West, I have to learn these things."

"Why, I—I never wanted to come to this wicked land!" she snapped. "Go and ask your father. I know what he'll say anyway." She ducked back into the wagon and whipped the canvas flaps shut.

James exchanged looks with Scott and Cady, then rode to the front of the wagon, where Mr. Walker was watering his oxen. He gave his permission for the lesson.

James helped Scott and Cady onto Corncob's back behind him. Corncob carried the three of them easily—together they couldn't have weighed much more than a big man like Pierre Delaroux.

James was a little embarrassed to have Cady's arms wrapped around his chest. She was a *girl*, after all, even if she didn't act like one most of the time.

They rode away from the trail to the open plains, where there would be plenty of room. The land stretched out endlessly around them. The air was so hot, it felt warm in James's nostrils. When they came to a wide area clear of the grass and low scrub that dotted the country, they dismounted.

"First you have to know how to get on a horse," said James.

He put his left foot in the stirrup, grabbed the saddle horn, and swung his right leg over Corncob's rump. "Easy, see?"

It wasn't so easy. Corncob stood patiently while Scott and Cady took turns sliding under the saddle or pitching over the far side.

"I guess it's not as simple as I thought it was," James observed.

"I guess not!" Cady exclaimed as she tumbled to the ground for the fourth time.

Finally both she and Scott were able to mount Corncob without too much ruckus. The dismounts took care of themselves, though James would have preferred to see them land on their feet instead of on their backsides.

"City folk!" he muttered to himself.

"I heard that!" Cady shot back. "I'd like to see a

hayseed like you make it in Philadelphia. Broad Street eats your kind alive!"

James laughed. "You may be right, Cady. If we ever go to Philadelphia, you can teach me about the city," he said. "But right now you're in the country, so you have to listen to me. And you two are doing fine. Really."

The lesson continued, with James showing them how to move up and down in rhythm to Corncob's walk and trot.

"I'm so rattled, I feel like my teeth are gonna fall out," Scott joked.

"You have to move with her," said James. "It just takes practice. Soon you'll be so smooth, you'll be able to balance a glass of water on your head at a full gallop."

James showed them how to canter.

"The canter's easier than the trot," he explained as he rode around them. "It's faster, but it's a lot less jouncy."

Scott went first, urging Corncob into a loping canter. He circled around James and Cady a few times, then whoaed Corncob to a halt. He was grinning broadly. "That was fun!"

"You're really getting the hang of it," James said.

Next it was Cady's turn. She cantered Corncob around for a minute, then shouted, "Is this all? Can't she run any faster?"

"Why, sure she can," James said, "but I don't think you should—"

Cady kicked her heels hard into Corncob's sides. The horse neighed loudly and broke into a gallop. Cady lost her grip on the reins and fell back in the saddle. "Whoa!" she cried, but Corncob was already taking off.

"Cady, wait!" James yelled. Corncob was galloping away from them, in the direction of the open plains. James cracked up laughing. "C'mon, Scott. Let's go get 'em."

"What're you laughing at?" Scott said, shocked. "That horse is running away with my little sister!"

"Oh, they won't get far. Corncob's an old nag. When she tires, she'll stop. And when Corncob decides to stop, she's stubborner than a mule about starting up again."

James and Scott ran after Cady, who was busy kicking and screaming for help at the top of her lungs—not the best way to get a horse to slow down. But sure enough, after about a mile of galloping, Corncob came to an abrupt halt. Cady hopped off quickly.

She tried to lead Corncob back, but the horse wouldn't budge. So Cady had to stand there red faced while the boys came to her.

James and Scott ran up, laughing raucously.

"Hoo, hoo! You should've heard yourself!" James said. *"Help! Whoa! Help!"* he screeched.

"You didn't tell me this horse was a lunatic!" Cady shouted.

Corncob looked at her placidly.

"What was the big idea kicking her like that?" James asked. "I hadn't shown you how to gallop yet."

Cady lifted her chin proudly. "I wanted to do something Scott hadn't done."

"Well, you sure succeeded," Scott said, wheezing. He was breathing heavily from the run and the belly laugh.

"You all right, Scott?" Cady asked, her face serious.

"I'm fine—fine."

A chill was coming over the air. The sky in the west was a bright red and orange, and the sun was nearing the horizon.

"We best be getting back," James said. "Scott, why don't you ride Corncob. She looks pretty beat. The cavalry and I will walk."

Dusk was coming on, and the three were in a hurry to get back to the train. Corncob, however, would not be rushed. She was tired from the day's journey and the strenuous gallop, and refused to move faster than a slow walk. Luckily, sunset was lighter than usual because a full moon was rising in the east.

Then James heard a dog bark.

The hairs on the back of his neck stood on end.

What would a dog be doing in the middle of the plains all by himself?

There was another bark, and a low howl.

"What was that, James?" Cady asked quietly.

"I'm not sure, but I have a bad feeling . . ." he started. Then he saw a large gray-and-white wolf come up out of a shallow creekbed.

"James?" Scott whispered.

"Shhh," James hushed him. He wished he'd brought a gun.

Corncob whinnied softly, and Scott patted her neck.

The gray-and-white wolf was followed by another, darker wolf, and then another, and another. Soon more than twenty wolves were loping around, yelping, sniffing at Corncob, whining, nipping at each other. Their pointy ears and faces weren't very different from those of many dogs James had seen. But the wolves were bigger and shaggier than any dog. Their eyes glowed green and blue in the moonlight.

The three children stood as still as possible. Corncob pranced and snorted in fear. James saw her eyes rolling up into her head, and froth forming around her bit. He knew if she kicked out at one of the wolves, it would all be over for them.

"Hold her steady, Scott," he said between his teeth. "Don't let her bolt."

Scott tightened his grip on the reins and made

soothing sounds into Corncob's ears.

"What d'you think they mean to do?" Cady whispered.

"I don't know," James hissed. "Now hush up and don't panic."

A large black wolf with a bushy tail sat down and lifted his muzzle to the sky. He let out a long, mournful howl. It was the eeriest thing James had ever heard.

Another one sat and howled, and soon four or five were howling in a chorus. The other wolves scampered around and yelped. James noticed there were some pups among them. He would have thought they were cute if he hadn't been terrified of their parents.

Then James saw two dark figures approaching from the direction of the wagon train. Colonel Stewart must have sent some men out to look for them when night fell and they hadn't returned. He breathed a sigh of relief. But what could two men, even with guns, do against twenty wolves?

As the men got closer, James's feeling of relief vanished completely. He could see that they weren't wearing shirts, and they carried bows instead of guns.

*Indians!*

"Land of mercy . . ." Cady murmured.

The two men were coming straight for them. The wolf pack parted to let them through. The pups romped playfully, and the sitting wolves never stopped howling.

Each man was walking steadily and holding a hand out near his hip. Some of the wolves trotted over to them and sniffed their hands. A couple even licked them.

The Indians were right beside the children now. They were tall and had long black hair and clean-shaven faces. They wore necklaces of beads and feathers. James knew they weren't Kaws or Potawatomi. He hoped they weren't Pawnee. He'd heard the Pawnee were cruel to their prisoners.

Without a word one man took James and Cady by the hands while the other grasped Corncob's bridle. Cady gave a little cry, but Corncob seemed to welcome the touch. The Indians started to lead them forward.

James took a breath and braced himself for the worst. He expected to feel a wolf's sharp teeth on his throat at any second.

But the pack was unconcerned as the people and horse left its circle. The wolves went on yapping and playing and howling.

Neither James nor Cady nor Scott said anything as the Indians led them on. James was wondering if he'd ever see his family again. Were the Indians planning to kill them or hold them hostage? He'd heard rumors of Indians stealing children from wagon trains and raising them as their own. He wondered what his new family would be like.

James blinked back tears and shivered from the cold. He heard Cady's soft whimpering and Scott's nervous gasps for breath. Only Corncob seemed at ease. She was tossing her head and walking with a springy step.

Then James saw the glow from the wagon train's campfires. Were these Indians planning to trade them for goods here and now? What would he be worth?

Suddenly the Indian released James's hand. The other man let go of Corncob. It was only then that James realized the Indians had brought them to safety and were letting them go. They slipped into the deepening shadows and disappeared without a word.

"Wait!" James called after them. "Where are you going? We want to thank you."

No sound came back except the distant howling of the wolves. Corncob shook her mane and started forward again. James knew she wanted her evening meal.

"Let's go on, then," James said to Cady and Scott. They shuffled forward wearily. "I guess you're going to catch it from your ma," he commented as they drew near the wagons.

Cady and Scott said nothing.

And James didn't utter another word until he felt the delicious heat of a campfire on his face.

# TWELVE

## THE BUFFALO HUNT

Their families had been worried sick when James, Cady, and Scott weren't back by sundown. They feared the children were in trouble, especially when they heard wolves howling in the distance. But Colonel Stewart refused to allow a search party to go out. He'd said it was too dangerous.

When the children finally did return, the emigrants were amazed to hear their story. Some didn't believe it. The wolf pack would have torn them apart in an instant, they argued.

Then a voice rang out of the darkness: "Wicked, wicked land!" The crowd around the children fell quiet. James saw Mrs. Walker stride into the light of the campfire.

"I told them not to leave the wagon," she said to no one in particular. "I told them not to enter the wilderness." She had on the same severe black dress she always wore. James could tell from her red eyes and mussed hair that she'd been crying. She was clutching a Bible against her chest.

"'A lion out of the forest shall slay them!'" she hissed, raising the Bible above her head. "'A wolf of the evenings shall spoil them; every one that goeth out thence shall be torn in pieces!'"

James recognized the words as a verse from the Bible, but he had no idea which chapter they came from. He glanced over at Scott and Cady. They looked stricken by the sight of their mother in such a state.

Mrs. Walker stood like a statue, the Bible in her trembling, upraised hand, until her husband gently lowered her arm. "Rebecca, dear, come now," he said softly. "The children are unharmed. Let's get some rest. We've all had too much excitement for one day." Mr. Walker led his wife and children away.

Pierre Delaroux broke the uneasy silence that followed. "I believe the children." He was picking up the earlier argument where it had left off. "Wolves eat when they are hungry. When they are not hungry . . . good, the children are lucky. But tomorrow, maybe not so lucky."

Then Jenson Carver spoke up. "I don't know about wolves, but I'd bet my right hand them Indians didn't let the young'uns go on purpose."

"How do you mean, Mr. Carver?" James's pa asked.

"I mean they accidentally took 'em too close to the wagons and got scared and ran away. They'd've scalped 'em if they'd got the chance."

"That's not true!" James exclaimed. "They saved us from—"

"Jamie," Pa said mildly. "Mind your elders." He turned to Carver. "I believe the boy is right, sir. Those Indians weren't intending my son and his friends any harm. Why, they risked their own lives to help them."

"You can believe that if it makes you feel better, mister," said Carver. "I know what I know."

"Well, all I can say is I'm glad they were there," Pa concluded.

"And what d'you think they was doing so near the train, anyways?" Carver asked the crowd assembled around the fire. His eyes fixed on Colonel Stewart.

"By the children's description," Colonel Stewart said mildly, "I'd say they were Pawnee."

James's eyes bugged out. Pawnee? They were bloodthirsty killers! The men who'd helped them hadn't seemed like savages.

"I'm sure those two men were just scouts," Colonel Stewart continued. "The Pawnee have been watching us for some time now."

"Some time!" Carver exploded. "Some time? Why

wasn't we told about this? We need to be ready for 'em when they attack."

Some of the men around the campfire muttered in agreement.

"It was Pawnee started the stampede that nearly killed ever'body," said Carver, trying to whip up the crowd. James didn't remember seeing Carver out on the lines with the other men when the buffalo stampeded.

There was more grumbling from the men. "Why weren't we alerted to 'em, Colonel?" one asked.

"I did inform some of the men that the Pawnee had their eye on us," he responded.

James saw his pa nod. He had known and hadn't said anything!

"But I saw no need to alarm each and every man," Colonel Stewart added. "Especially hotheads like your Mr. Carver. We weren't even in Pawnee country when the buffalo stampeded. It's utter foolishness to say the Pawnee started it. They won't attack us for no reason. I've ridden this trail before. As long as we pass through their lands peacefully, they'll leave us be."

Pierre Delaroux stepped up beside Colonel Stewart. He placed his hand on his pistol. "The colonel is correct. If you fools provoke the Pawnees, you will live to regret it." He looked around at the men's angry faces glowing in the firelight. "Or, perhaps, you will not live to regret it."

With that he and the colonel left the circle. The men broke up, saying they had to get an early start in the morning. Then James heard Carver mutter something about them Indians being no better'n dead dogs in the street.

He was certain no good could come of such talk.

A few days later, Colonel Stewart organized the first buffalo hunt. A small herd had been spotted some miles to the north. Pierre Delaroux would lead the group. Few of the men were experienced hunters. The only ones who'd ever shot an animal as large as a buffalo were those who'd fought off the stampede two weeks before.

Delaroux asked for volunteers, men who were good shots and good horsemen. James watched as seven men came forward, including his brother and his pa.

Since Jeremy had saved Pa's life, he'd been taking a more active role in the wagon train. He and Will had even struck up a friendship. James was glad to see that his brother was less unhappy now than he'd been at the start of the trip.

Pa got his fifty-caliber Hawken rifle, shot, and power. He put an old flintlock pistol in his belt and commenced saddling up Mackie.

"Can I come along, Pa?" James asked.

"I'm afraid not, son," Pa replied. "It's too dangerous."

"Aw, let him come, Pa," said Jeremy. "He can ride with me on Corncob. I'll make sure he stays out of trouble." He patted the rifle lying across his lap. "I know how to handle a buffalo." James knew Jeremy was enjoying the role of his pa's savior.

"Jeremy, I'm not sure I'm even gonna allow you, let alone Jamie, to—" Pa paused, considering. Then he smiled and scratched his beard. "Maybe you two are old enough to take care of yourselves. After all, I was the one who got trampled by the buffalo."

"Great!" James shouted.

"But stay away from wolves, you hear me, boy?" Pa added. "Next time there may not be any friendly Indians to come along and rescue you."

James wished Cady and Scott could come on the hunt, but he knew Mrs. Walker would never allow it. They were restricted to the wagon for the time being, and anyway, Scott was feeling ill. He'd been coughing a lot lately and had even spit up some blood.

James wrapped his arms around Jeremy and held on tight as they followed the men north. It took the hunters over an hour to ride just the few miles to the buffalo. Most of the horses were slow farm animals like Mackie and Corncob, and all of them were tired from the weeks' journey. James imagined how exciting it would be to ride a fast, hot-blooded horse like he knew Bolt would be. It wouldn't be long before he and Bolt would be flying past these plodding old workhorses.

He would give Cady more riding lessons, despite what her mother said. They were on the frontier now. Cady had to learn how to survive in the country. He could tell she was a natural rider, even if she had let Corncob run away with her. He'd give Scott lessons, too, when he was better. James wondered when that would be.

The hunters crested a low ridge and drew up sharp. Below them, about a quarter of a mile away, a herd of buffalo grazed. They seemed small and harmless, like gophers, so far away, but James knew they looked different up close.

Pierre Delaroux divided the men into two groups. James and Jeremy stuck with their pa. Their group was to circle around north of the herd. The other group, which included Will and Delaroux, was to approach the herd from the east. Each group was to agree in advance on one animal to fire at.

"It's almost impossible to kill buffalo with a single bullet," Delaroux explained. "Such a shot is one in a thousand—more luck than skill." He glanced at Jeremy, who shifted in the saddle. "We are not greedy. We work together, or we kill nothing except, perhaps, each other. Agreed?"

The men nodded.

"Good. Now, on my signal, fire at the buffalo you have chosen. Aim for this spot." Delaroux reached over his shoulder and patted himself on the back. "If he falls, is good, is done. If he is merely wounded . . . ah, well, mount your horses and ride after him." He shrugged. "And good luck to you, my friends."

Pa, Jeremy, James, and two other men rode around to the north and dismounted. They had to be off their horses in order to sneak up on the herd. The men loaded their rifles and crept through the low scrub. Far off to the left, James could see Delaroux's men approaching the herd. The wind was out of the west, so the buffalo would not sense either group coming.

The animals seemed peaceful and contented as they munched lazily at the sparse grass, swishing their tails back and forth to ward off flies. They looked as defenseless as fat jersey heifers in a green Pennsylvania pasture.

But James knew it was an illusion. The buffalo were big and strong, with sharp horns and hooves— and there were so many of them. Even a small herd like this one had several hundred animals in it. A wolf pack might be able to catch a wandering calf every now and then, but a full-grown buffalo in a herd had no enemies.

James had been told that before the settlers came with their horses and guns, even the Indians had had no easy way of killing a buffalo. A group of men on foot, with just bows and arrows for weapons, was no match for a thousand thundering beasts. The

Indians used to stampede them off cliffs. James would like to have seen that. And he had to admire the Indians' ingenuity.

The hunters were creeping slowly now. They were within a hundred feet of the herd. James saw the six men motion silently among themselves toward a large bull. That was the one they'd go for. James wished his pa had let him take a gun.

One by one, all the men except Pa raised their rifles to their shoulders and sighted the big bull. Pa was looking over toward Delaroux, waiting for the signal. James could feel the tension in the air. The wind rustled in the grass. A fly circled his head and buzzed off. A grasshopper trilled.

Then James saw Delaroux fling his arm up, and simultaneously four puffs of white rose from the rifles in the other group.

*"Now!"* Pa whispered as he smoothly swung his rifle around toward the bull.

*Cra-a-ack!* Three shots went off all together. James saw the big bull stumble, while all around it buffalo were off and running in the opposite direction. A moment later and—*crack!*—Pa fired, and the bull fell to its front knees.

Blood was streaming from behind the bull's shoulder, right where Delaroux had told the men to aim for. The bull's hind legs were driving forward, but its huge head and front legs were dragging in the dirt.

It tried to lift itself up, but—*crack!* Jeremy had reloaded and fired again. The bull was back to its knees. *Cra-ack!* The other hunters fired together, and the bull collapsed. Its tail swished a few times, and then the great brown body was still.

"Yahoo!" James yelled, leaping up. "Got 'im!" He pounded Jeremy on the back, then hugged his pa hard around the chest. The other hunters were whooping and slapping each other with their hats.

Will's group had downed its buffalo also. James thought the smile on Delaroux's face was the first one he'd seen that wasn't meant to be threatening.

The dead buffalo were far too big to butcher out on the plains. The men tied them around the hooves and took turns walking while their horses dragged the carcasses back to the wagons.

James had never felt so proud as when Elizabeth and his ma came running up to greet the returning hunters. They put up quite a to-do over Jeremy, Pa, and him. James told them to stop with the fussing, it was all in a day's work, but secretly he was pleased. He could tell Pa and Jeremy were too.

And his brother didn't even remind them that James hadn't fired a shot.

James looked at the huge animal his group had killed. It would feed half the wagon train for a week. The hide would keep a sick person like Scott warm during the long cold nights. James had helped provide for his family. He felt like a hero. Like a man.

## THIRTEEN

## CYCLONE!

"**T**his is the Platte?" James exclaimed. He was walking with his pa and Pierre Delaroux. "I thought we were going to see a great big river like the Missouri. This is just an overgrown creek."

The Platte was wide, shallow, and muddy, the color of milky coffee. Not a fish jumped, not a duck paddled in the murky sludge. The current was so slow, the river seemed not to be moving at all.

"It's not what I expected either, Jamie," said Pa. "Maybe it's more impressive upriver."

Delaroux broke into another of his loud, hooting laughs. "Ah, you're a good man, Mr. Gregg, but you know nothing about the West. Why do you think she is called the Platte?"

James and Pa looked quizzically at Delaroux.

"Platte? Platte?" Delaroux laughed out loud. "Is

French for *flat*, no? And that she is. Very flat. They say of this river she is too thick to drink, too thin to plow. And get used to the sight of her—we will see her for many weeks."

In the distance, on the far, northern side of the Platte, dust rose over the wagons of emigrants coming from Iowa along the Mormon Trail. The Mormons were followers of a man named Brigham Young, who was leading the persecuted religious group to a place in the desert called Mormon City, near the Great Salt Lake.

James had been told the Mormons would be in sight, off and on, all the way to Fort Laramie, where the Mormon Trail joined the Oregon Trail. A couple hundred miles beyond Fort Laramie, at Fort Bridger, the Mormons would leave the Oregon Trail to continue south to Mormon City.

The days along the Platte were as unchanging as the river itself. Wagons broke down, the wooden wheels shrinking in the sun and dry air until their metal rims popped off in the hot dust. Animals weakened and broke down as well. Grazing was not good. Tempers flared among the emigrants. Many fell ill from drinking the sour waters of the river.

James's feet were blistered, his lips cracked from the heat and dust. Yet still he trudged on uncomplaining. He was too proud to ride in the wagon and be an additional burden on the family's weary oxen.

Jeremy came down with a bad case of dysentery.

Emigrants were known to have dropped dead in their tracks from the loss of body fluids. Ma forced him to spend a few days resting in the back of the wagon.

Not even Will smiled and joked as much. He was spending most of his time with the Jenningtons. He helped Sara's father drive the team, and looked after their dozen sheep. James knew he was doing it so he could be around Sara.

Scott was feeling very ill. He'd come down with dysentery, too, and what with his weak lungs, he was hardly able to leave the wagon. Not that Mrs. Walker would have allowed it anyway.

James suspected Mrs. Walker was not fit herself. She was constantly muttering over her Bible. James knew there was nothing so odd in that—James's ma read aloud from the Bible every night before they went to sleep. But Ma read the nice parts, about wise men building their houses on rocks, and angels coming upon shepherds, and lilies of the valley. Mrs. Walker always talked about transgressions and God's judgments and pestilences and plagues.

Cady had told James about how her mother would hardly speak to her father except to call him a sinner or a backslider. And Mrs. Walker left the wagon less often than Scott did. James wondered how Scott would ever get better with his ma filling him up with all that talk of wounded cries and bitter wailings.

The only one who seemed to be thriving on the trail was Bolt. James watered and fed him every day, and though the grass was sparse and the water muddy, Bolt grew stronger. During nooning Cady would sneak away from her mother, and she would help James groom him. Bolt whinnied with pleasure when they brushed the road dust off him. His speckled gray coat shone with a healthy gleam.

One day Mr. Meacham came around during nooning. James was showing Cady the proper way to curry Bolt. Meacham looked the horse up and down, rubbing his bony chin with his hands. "You done mighty fine with my horse there, boy," he said to James.

"*Your* horse?" James said.

"That's right. I believe I let you play with him long enough. Now, missy," he said to Cady, "if you'll just hand over them reins . . ."

Cady shot a look at James, who quickly took the reins from her.

"Now, boy," Meacham started, "I'm sure you was misunderstandin' me when I loaned him to you."

James stared at the man in astonishment. "You *gave* him to me!" he burst out. He'd never in his life spoken to an adult this way, but no adult had ever tried to cheat him.

"Gave him to you? Now, why would I do a thing like that? I'd have to be a fool to give away such a fine piece of horseflesh." Meacham narrowed his eyes. "And if you said I did, who'd take the word of a squirt like you?"

James couldn't believe his ears. "You dirty, no-good, lying, cheating sku—"

"James!" Will Gantry appeared from behind the Greggs' wagon. He had heard the whole conversation. "Now, Mr. Meacham, you'd best be on your way," he said in an exaggerated drawl, stepping toward him. "I was there when you gave this honest young man the horse. I saw it with my own eyes and heard it with my own ears, and I'm not afraid to say so." His nose was within six inches of Meacham's. "And I do believe Colonel Stewart will take the word of a squirt like me."

Will stared hard at Meacham till the older man spun on his heels. "You won't git away with cheatin' me like this, you yellow whelps!" he shouted over his shoulder.

Will chuckled as he watched Meacham stalk off. James was still so angry, he couldn't speak.

"What d'you reckon he's planning on doing, Will?" Cady asked.

"Who, Meacham? Aw, nothing. He's just mad 'cause James here saw something in a sickly colt that nobody else did." He slapped James on the shoulder. "Don't you worry about Meacham, Jamie. No one's gonna take Bolt away from you."

James was reassured by Will's words. But he

couldn't help feeling that he hadn't seen the last of old Mr. Meacham.

That afternoon the sky darkened early in the west. It had been over a week since the emigrants had had any rain. The mood of the train lifted as the rain clouds formed. Even a heavy storm like the one they'd had the first day out would be better than another dry, dusty evening.

Colonel Stewart rode up and down the train, barking out orders. By now the emigrants were so practiced at forming the nightly circle that the whole operation took less than half an hour. On this day, however, Colonel Stewart was in a particular hurry.

"I don't like the looks of those clouds!" he shouted to Pa. The wind was picking up already. "Tie down everything you can, and say good-bye to everything you can't tie. We're in for a blow." He rode to the next wagon, shouting, "Tie down! Tie down!"

James and Jeremy scurried around, hammering picket lines for the horses and oxen as quickly as they could. Ma and Elizabeth were binding ropes over the canvas top of the wagon. James knew the storm was going to be a bad one when he saw his pa strapping the wheels of the wagon to stakes in the ground.

"Better safe than sorry," Pa said. "I heard tell of whole wagons lifted off the ground in these blows."

The first fat raindrops fell, sending up little puffs of dust where they hit the ground.

"Sam! Jeremy! Jamie!" Ma called. She was holding Elizabeth tight against her side. "Get under the wagon now!"

The family ducked under just in time. The clouds fell open, spilling rain like they'd been saving it up for weeks. The parched, dusty ground was a sea of mud in a matter of seconds.

But after only a few minutes the rain started letting up.

"That's it?" James asked, almost disappointed.

"I hope so, son," said Pa. "Though I don't think it's over yet."

In another few minutes the rain had almost stopped. People all around the circle were emerging from their wagons.

James got out and peered at the sky. The air was strangely calm. In the west the sun was setting and the clouds were a dull red. But nearer, almost overhead, James saw that the sky was a weird greenish hue mixed with purple and brown.

The clouds were swirling around, and every now and then they seemed to dip down for an instant before shooting back up again.

James noticed that everyone was watching the sky. Only a few seconds ago they were laughing and shouting at the shortness of the storm. Now they were stone silent.

113

The clouds curled and whipped, and there were flashes of lightning in the greenest, ugliest part. Still no rain fell on the emigrants, and the air remained calm, almost deathly. All the force of the storm seemed collected in the whirling, dipping clouds overhead.

Then a spinning light-gray column dropped down out of the ceiling of green and purple clouds. It dangled for a moment, then reached all the way to the ground. Instantly a sinister dark-brown color shot back up the column from the base.

*"Cyclone!"* someone shouted.

The emigrants, who a moment before had been as still as the air, scattered in all directions. The wind, too, was suddenly in motion.

James stood mesmerized by the towering brown funnel as it wandered erratically across the plain. The air shrieked and howled around him, but he was strangely calm. He knew that unlike a herd of buffalo, there was no fighting off a cyclone. If it came their way, they were done for. They were powerless to stop it.

He felt as he had when he'd stood on the ridge and watched the vast herd of buffalo gallop toward the horizon. The land was vast, too vast for people ever to tame it. In a thousand years these plains would still be empty but for the Indians. Like the buffalo and the plains themselves, the cyclone was beautiful in its ruthlessness.

Amid the yelling of the people and howling of the wind, James alone was at peace. He knew he would never forget this moment.

That is, if he lived to remember it.

James heard a crash, and turned to see the Walkers' wagon toppled over on its side. Mr. Walker must not have tied it down securely enough.

He ran over to help them. Scott and Cady were watching as their father dragged Mrs. Walker out of the overturned wagon. She was stabbing her finger at a page of the Bible, screaming over and over, "'Behold, the whirlwind of the Lord goeth forth with fury! It shall fall upon the heads of the wicked!'"

Cady and Scott stood by helplessly, holding each other and crying. They were pleading with their mother to stop.

James knew he had to get them away from there. He grabbed them by the arms. "She'll be fine!" he hollered over the wind. "Your pa'll care for her! Come with me!"

He dragged Cady and Scott to his own wagon, where his family crouched beneath it.

"James!" his ma called. Her face, usually so rosy, was blanched with fear. "Where have you been? Come here!" She jumped out from under the wagon, grabbed James, Scott, and Cady, and smothered all three of them in a long hug. "You'll be the death of me yet, you rascal!" she said to James, and hugged them again.

"Where's your folks?" James's ma asked Cady and Scott. When they didn't answer, she smiled and said, "Doesn't matter. You just stay here with us till the storm's over."

She gathered the three children in her arms and hustled them toward the wagon.

"I have to check on Bolt, Ma," James said, wrestling free. She gave him an exasperated look, but let him go.

James ran to his horse. Bolt appeared nervous, but he hadn't been panicked by the wind. He wasn't nearly as jumpy as he had been the last time they'd had a storm. James patted him and talked to him for a while.

He saw that the cyclone was farther away now. It was heading north, away from the wagons. The plains had chosen to spare them, at least this time.

Jeremy and Pa came running up to check on Mackie, Corncob, and the other animals. All were fine.

The wind had died down enough so that they didn't have to shout anymore. The cyclone was a mile to the north and receding fast.

"Mrs. Walker's not gonna make it, is she, Pa?" James asked.

"We don't know that, son," Pa said. "Sometimes people find a hidden strength inside them that no one knew they had."

James considered Pa's words. He looked at his brother soothing Corncob and calmly watching the

116

storm. Some folks would say Jeremy had found a hidden strength inside. James hoped his pa was right about Mrs. Walker. But as he watched the cyclone disappear into the distance and the gathering darkness, he couldn't help worrying about what would happen to Cady and Scott.

# FOURTEEN

## THE COLONEL'S COAT

That night the emigrants celebrated around a bonfire. They were happy it had stormed and even happier that the storm hadn't killed them.

Two wagons in addition to the Walkers' had blown over. But no one was hurt, and the wagons weren't damaged badly. No livestock had bolted— the emigrants were much better at tying down their animals than they had been when they started the journey. Also, the animals were wearier and less inclined to run off.

James sat with Cady, Scott, and Jeremy. Will and Sara Jennington were nearby. Colonel Stewart was telling the emigrants about storms he'd seen that were much worse.

"Why, I remember one rainstorm—'thirty-seven, I believe it was, back in New York—it was raining so

119

hard, we had to dive into Lake Erie to keep from drowning!"

Everyone laughed, even Cady and Scott. James was surprised to see Colonel Stewart telling jokes—he was usually so stern.

Then Will spoke up. "Aw, those old Yankee rainstorms are nothing compared to the weather we get in Virginia. Listen to this—one summer it was so hot, the corn in the fields popped off the ears."

James and the others whooped.

"But that's not all," Will continued. "When my daddy's old dog saw that white all over the ground, he thought it was snow and fell over frozen to death!"

Then Sara piped up. "Frozen to death? In Virginia? Why, in Massachusetts, where I come from, it gets so cold, your shadow freezes right to the ground. One time I saw a pond freeze over so quick, the ducks got stuck in the ice. That night they flapped their wings and flew away, leaving just a big hole in the ground."

That brought the biggest laugh of all. James wished he knew some stories he could tell about the weather in Pennsylvania. But all he could think of were the gentle spring mornings and crisp fall afternoons. Suddenly a wave of homesickness washed over him.

"My, my, we have some storytellers to match wits with tonight," Colonel Stewart said. "But I wonder if Mr. Gantry and Miss Jennington have seen all the things they claim to have, or if they're just telling tales." Suddenly his voice grew serious. "What I'm about to tell you really happened to me."

The people around the fire grew quiet. The colonel began in a soft, low voice. "It was on my last crossing. Myself and another fellow, name of Hank Jackson, were up in the Bitterroots. Must've been six, seven thousand feet up. We were on our way to meet some trappers.

"We come upon this Indian fellow. He'd been caught in a slide—arm was all busted up. He's weak and bleeding, shivering from the cold and pain. It was a pitiful sight. Well, Jackson and I, we can't just leave him there to die all alone on the mountain. So I wrap him in my old blue coat, and we load him up on a mule and bring him down.

"By the time we got off the mountain, night was coming on. The Indian motions for us to take a spur off the trail. Jackson spoke a little of the Indian's language. He says the man wants us to take him to his village. Sure enough, not a hundred yards on we see the twinkling lights of a village through the trees.

"Then the Indian tells Jackson to drop him there. Well, we're puzzled, but the man insists, so we do what he says. He stumbles off toward his village, and we go back to the trail. It wasn't till the next day I remembered I'd given the man my coat."

Colonel Stewart paused.

"That's an interesting tale, sir," Will said, "but I can't say as I see how it's more fantastic than Sara's flying pond."

That got a small laugh, which the colonel cut off by saying, "The story's not over yet." He glared at the folks around the fire, and spoke at nearly a whisper. "Well, Jackson and I did our trading with the trappers. On the way back, we were passing by the spur to the Indian village when it occurs to me we should see how the man's doing. So we ride up, and Jackson tells the people we're the fellows who carried the injured man off the mountain.

"Well, they tell Jackson they don't know what we're talking about. There's no injured man in the village. Now, you can imagine our consternation. 'Sure there is,' Jackson says, and he describes the man, what he looked like. The Indians say they don't know him.

"Then this little old wrinkled squaw comes up. She's been listening the whole time. 'You've seen my grandfather,' she says.

"'Grandfather?' Jackson says. 'That can't be. The man we helped couldn't've been more'n forty, and your grandfather must be a hundred if he's a day—that's assuming he's still alive.'

"'Oh no,' says the squaw. 'My grandfather isn't alive. He died in a rock slide on the mountain sixty years ago, when I was just a little girl. You saw his spirit.'"

Colonel Stewart looked from face to face. No one was laughing now.

"Jackson and I, we weren't convinced. So that old squaw takes us to see her grandpap's grave. We were the first white men ever to set foot in the holy burial ground. And when we get there, what do you suppose we find?"

James shivered. He had no idea, but he hoped it wasn't a ghost. He noticed Sara reach over for Will's hand, then quickly snatch her hand away again.

Colonel Stewart leaned forward. "Draped across the grave of the squaw's grandfather," he whispered, "was my old blue coat!"

There was a silence, broken only by the crackling of the campfire and a nervous cough or two. "That was a good one, Colonel," somebody said.

"Yeah," said someone else. "So good, I don't think I'll be able to sleep tonight."

Everybody laughed nervously. Colonel Stewart stood up abruptly. "I best be turning in," he announced. "Early start tomorrow, you know." He started walking away from the fire. Then he turned. "Oh, and one other thing. That coat I gave the old squaw's grandfather?" He patted his chest. "It's the very one I have on now." And with that he disappeared into the darkness.

No one said anything for a moment. Then Scott whispered, "I sure wouldn't touch anything a spirit had worn."

123

"Me neither," said Cady. She turned to James. "You think all that really happened to the colonel?"

"Naw," James answered. "'Course not. That's just a story he made up. I bet he never met any injured Indian in the mountains." James wished he was as sure of himself as he sounded.

Mr. Walker felt it would be best if his children stayed with the Greggs for the night. He had to repair the wagon and care for his wife. Pa and Ma agreed.

When Cady and Scott piled into James and Jeremy's tent, Jeremy grumbled about being overrun by pups. But James could tell he was glad for the extra company. He'd been spooked by the colonel's tale, too.

James closed his eyes and listened to the slow breathing of his brother and his two friends. All he could think about was the colonel's coat rising up into the air on the back of an Indian spirit and flying over the wagon train.

It was nearly dawn before he fell asleep.

# FIFTEEN

## FRONTIER JUSTICE

The Pawnee kept their distance, but they were watching the emigrants. Once, James spotted a Pawnee scout on horseback, silhouetted on a ridge. Another time he saw two on foot, crouched behind an outcrop of rock. After the incident with the wolf pack, he wasn't convinced that the Pawnee were as bloodthirsty as everyone said they were.

Still, he never liked the sight of them.

One morning the emigrants passed the place where the north fork and the south fork of the Platte River joined. The train stuck to the south bank of the South Platte. Soon they would ford the South Platte, then cross overland to rejoin the North Platte. They'd follow it past Chimney Rock, to Fort Laramie, and beyond, to the Sweetwater River and the Rocky Mountains.

James was glad to be leaving Pawnee country, but

where they were heading was not much better: Dakotah, Crow, and Arapaho territory. Those Indians weren't supposed to be much friendlier than the Pawnee.

Suddenly a shot rang out ahead. James had been walking behind the family wagon. He ran up to his pa, who was driving the team.

"What happened, Pa?" he asked. The train had come to a halt.

"Don't rightly know, son," Pa replied. "But if it was a gunshot, it can't mean anything but trouble."

James trotted past five or six wagons to where a group of men were standing. They were arguing, and pointing to a clump of brush not far from the trail.

Colonel Stewart had ridden back from the head of the train and was demanding to know what had happened.

"I seen some Indians snooping around and decided to run 'em off," a man said. James recognized him as Jenson Carver.

"You decided to run them off, did you?" the colonel asked icily.

"They was up to no good," Carver insisted. "But I filled one of 'em with buckshot. That'll teach them redskins." He waved his shotgun at Colonel Stewart.

"Those men were Pawnee scouts, you fool. I told you I've been aware of them for weeks. We are trav-

126

eling through their lands. Of course they keep an eye on us! But they mean us no harm." The colonel shook his head. "I hope for all our sakes you're as bad a shot as you are a judge of Indians."

"I saw one fellow run up that way," said a man who'd been arguing with Carver earlier. He pointed to a low outcropping of rock. "I think there were two of 'em, though."

Colonel Stewart dismounted and led three men toward the bushes Carver had fired at.

James looked over at Carver, who was gripping his shotgun and muttering to himself. "This is the thanks I git for runnin' off them danged Indians. They was askin' for it, nosin' around the train, waitin' for a chance to grab our livestock an' womenfolk. . . ."

Colonel Stewart reappeared from behind the scrub. His face was grim. Then his three companions emerged from the bushes. They were carrying a wounded man. There was blood on the chest and stomach of the shirtless body. He was unarmed, without even bow and arrows.

James knew the wagon train was in danger now.

"I ain't scared of no Indians!" James heard somebody yell. "I say we fight 'em!"

There were loud shouts of approval, and even louder hisses and boos.

Although it was only midday, Colonel Stewart

127

had ordered the wagons into the nighttime circle. He had called a meeting of the entire train. By now the Pawnee who had been seen running away would have alerted his village. Soon every Pawnee for a hundred miles would know about the unprovoked attack.

The man Carver had shot was still alive, but just barely. He refused the food and water he was offered. He seemed determined to die rather than accept help from his assailants.

There were two things to decide. First, what to do with Jenson Carver. And second, what to do when the Pawnee came looking for revenge.

"I say we hang Carver now!" James heard one man shout. "I don't care if it was just an Indian. He shot a man, and he's gotta pay for it!"

Carver was bound hand and foot. He looked like he was ready to faint from fear, but Pierre Delaroux propped him up.

"Let him go!" someone else yelled. James saw a small grin break across Carver's haggard features. "We'll need every man behind a gun when the Pawnee come. Afterward we can hang 'im." Carver's face sagged.

James's pa spoke up. "Mr. Carver should be taken to Fort Laramie and turned over to the army. The man deserves a fair trial, and he can't get one here on the trail."

There were murmurs of agreement, plus some

grumbles of "Hang him!" and "Let him go!"

"Please . . ." Carver whispered hoarsely. "I didn't mean no harm. . . . I was protecting us all. . . . I beg of you . . ."

Then Delaroux released his grip on Carver, who collapsed facedown on the ground. "Your ideas of justice, Mr. Gregg, are admirable," Delaroux said. "But one way or the other, Mr. Carver, he will never see Fort Laramie."

Carver groaned and rolled over in the dust. "Please . . ." he croaked.

"And why is that, Mr. Delaroux?" Pa asked, ignoring the writhing prisoner.

"Simple," Delaroux said. "If we hang him now, he is dead. And the Pawnee attack, and we are dead too. If we do *not* hang him, and we try instead to take him to Fort Laramie, he is not dead. But the Pawnee still attack, and we are dead. And so, you see, is he. Good?"

"Not so good," Pa said, "but I see your point. What do you suggest we do?"

"You want Mr. Carver to get justice, yes?"

Pa nodded.

"And you want your family to see Fort Laramie, yes?"

Pa nodded again, more vigorously this time. James wondered what Delaroux was getting at.

"Is very clear. Mr. Carver did not shoot an army officer. So I say, what has the army at Fort Laramie to do with him? Nothing. Our foolish friend here shot a Pawnee Indian. And the Pawnee, they have their own justice. . . ."

James finally understood what Delaroux was suggesting. He wanted to hand Carver over to the Indians!

Carver seemed to have gotten the idea too. "No . . ." he pleaded. "Don't hand me over to them savages. . . . You can't do that. . . . Please . . ."

Pa was scratching his beard and looking up at the sky. "Well now, Mr. Delaroux, I can see as there's a certain justice in that idea. I trust the Pawnee will give him all the mercy he deserves. And it does seem to me to be the only way any of us is going to get to Fort Laramie alive."

"Turn 'im over!" someone shouted.

"Let the Pawnee hang 'im!" yelled a second voice.

"Better him than us!" came a third.

Carver was writhing on the ground and moaning. Delaroux left the circle without another word. Colonel Stewart went with him.

James too had no heart to watch his fellow emigrants celebrate the decision. He remembered the man he'd seen shot on the streets of Independence. All bloody and wounded, just like the poor Indian. He wondered if the man who'd shot him would ever be brought to justice, as Jenson Carver was going to be.

James had heard enough of Jenson Carver's

pleas for mercy. So had his pa, and James followed him back to the wagon.

Late that afternoon a dozen or so Pawnee were spotted making camp on a nearby ridge. They weren't even trying to make their presence a secret. The emigrants knew that more were coming. And the Pawnee knew they knew it.

Just before sunset James watched Colonel Stewart ride up the steep hillside to the ridge. He went unarmed, leading two horses. On the first was the body of the Indian. He had died an hour earlier. He was wrapped in the colonel's long blue coat.

On the second horse rode Mr. Carver. His hands were tied behind his back. His head hung low. He looked as limp as the man he had shot to death.

Half an hour later Colonel Stewart rode back down. He was alone and unharmed. He'd given the Pawnee their dead companion, Mr. Carver, and the two horses.

James thought about the brave men who had saved him, Cady, and Scott from the wolf pack. He knew in his heart that Mr. Carver deserved whatever terrible fate awaited him at the hands of the Pawnee.

And James hoped the colonel's old blue coat would comfort the spirit of the dead Pawnee as much as it had the squaw's grandfather.

131

# Sixteen

## Across the Wild River

The night before, it had rained for hours, the water falling in sheets, soaking everything.

The emigrants had been clinging to the south bank of the South Platte for a week, following the rutted tracks of the thousands of wagons that had come before. At last the tracks veered to the right and plunged down to the water. Here the train would cross the river and head for the North Platte.

Colonel Stewart had said the crossing should be easy. The South Platte was wide but shallow. The wagons would be able to ford it.

But James could see that the rains had raised the waters. The current was swift, swifter than he'd ever seen the usually placid South Platte.

There wasn't enough timber in the surrounding countryside to build rafts, and the wagons were too loaded down to float. The emigrants would have to

133

ford the river—and hope for the best.

James watched with interest as the first wagon entered the river. Colonel Stewart himself rode alongside the team of oxen, driving them with a long whip.

Scott and Cady stood beside James on the bank. It was one of the few times Scott had been out of his family's wagon in recent weeks. He looked thin and pale. He reached down, scooped up a handful of water from the Platte, and splashed it on his face.

"Feels good," he said.

"As long as we don't have to taste it," said Cady.

"I bet I could swim across," James said.

"You may have to if your wagon rolls over," Scott remarked.

James saw the swirling waters push hard against the wagon. For a moment he thought it might tip. But the weight of the load kept it upright. When the first wagon made it safely across, Colonel Stewart waved the others forward. A second wagon drove into the river, then a third.

The wagons entered the water in three lines. They moved slowly. James's wagon was lined up on the right. Will and the Jenningtons were upriver, on the left. For some reason Will had a big silly grin on his face. What's got into him? James wondered.

"Jamie!" his ma called. "You come get in this wagon before we leave you behind!"

"You best be getting back to your ma, too," James told Scott and Cady. "She'll want you with her on the crossing."

Cady and Scott exchanged glances and trudged slowly toward their wagon. It was in the center line. James sprinted for his own.

Pa was on Mackie, driving the team. James, Jeremy, and Elizabeth sat in the wagon with Ma while Corncob and Bolt trotted behind on leads.

"This is fun!" Elizabeth shouted as they went into the water. James could feel the wagon sway and dip with the current.

"I'm glad you think so, pumpkin," said Ma. "I'll just be happy when we're on solid ground again."

"Don't worry, Ma," said Jeremy. "Pa knows what he's doing."

James sat on the back rail of the wagon, hanging on to the bent-hickory pole over which the canvas top was stretched. He leaned out over the rushing water.

"Be careful, Jamie," Ma said from behind him.

"Aw, I am," James assured her. He looked upriver. The Walkers' wagon was right beside his own.

"Hey, Cady!" he yelled. "Look at me!" He leaned farther out over the water. He felt someone gently take hold of his pant leg. His ma, just making sure.

Cady poked her head out the back of her own wagon. She waved at James. "That's nothing!" she shouted. "I can do better than that!" She stood on the rear rail of the wagon, facing the front, and leaned out backward over the river. James could see the muscles in her hands straining to grip the bent poles of the wagon top.

"Be careful, Cady!" he hollered.

"You aren't scared, are you, James?" Cady trilled, and leaned back even farther.

James wondered what Cady's ma was doing while she performed this dangerous stunt. Muttering over her Bible, probably.

All of a sudden Cady's wagon pitched sharply to the right, then back to the left.

"Look out!" James yelled.

But he could only watch in astonishment as Cady plunged headfirst backward into the river. For a horrifying second she was completely underwater. Then she surfaced, shrieking wildly and flailing her arms over her head.

James had to do something. He was vaguely aware of Scott and Mrs. Walker screaming in their wagon, and of Jeremy and his own ma calling out behind him. He was too busy watching for Cady to be distracted by the others.

The raging brown water hurled her downstream, toward James's wagon. Her head kept ducking under and then bobbing up again as she sputtered and tried to scream. He wasn't even sure she saw him, but he stretched out over the water as far as he could.

"Cady, take my hand!" he shouted.

But she went under and swept right past him.

"Cady!" he screamed.

Her yellow hair broke the surface some yards downstream.

"I'm coming, Cady! Hang on!" James went to dive out of the wagon, but his ma gripped his leg.

"Don't, Jamie!" she pleaded.

"She's gonna drown!" James shot Jeremy a look, and his brother took Ma gently by the shoulders. She eased back into his grasp and released James's leg.

He tumbled into the river.

James was momentarily shocked by the cold and quiet under water. He kicked downstream hard and pulled himself to the surface. Cady was less than thirty feet away.

"Hang on, Cady!" he managed to yell before taking in a mouthful of water. He coughed and gagged, paddling toward Cady as quickly as he could. The water was even rougher than it looked, though it wasn't very deep—James could feel the riverbed every now and then when he kicked.

Cady was thrashing less now and had stopped screaming altogether. It seemed all she could do to keep her head above water. And she was failing that more and more each second.

"I'm coming, Cady!" James called. "Just hang

on!" He lunged forward two, three times. He almost had her.

Cady went under.

Where was she? "Cady!" James screamed, then ducked his head. He couldn't see anything in the muddy brown water. He groped around where he thought the current was taking her. His hand felt something. A piece of cloth? Yes, it was the sleeve of her dress. He grabbed on to it and pulled it toward him.

James pushed off the silty river bottom and broke the surface, gasping for breath. He pulled Cady up by the shoulders so her head was above water, too.

She groaned and spat out a large quantity of brown water.

He felt her hold tight to his arm.

"We're gonna be fine," James said. She spat up again in response.

James kicked his legs hard and used his free arm to keep her above water. He was relieved that he'd caught hold of her in time. But the relief evaporated as he realized they were still very much in danger. The north bank was several hundred yards away, and the current was taking them farther and farther from the wagon train.

James swam as well as he could through the turbulent, icy water. The river was still too deep for him to stand up and walk, but his toes were touching bottom more often now.

138

The minutes passed, and they proceeded slowly to the north bank. Cady was almost limp in his arms—she wasn't helping with the swimming, but at least she did hang on to him.

James looked upriver. The wagon train was no longer in sight. He wondered idly how far downstream they'd come. If they stayed in the river long enough, they would wind up back in Independence. He would have laughed out loud at the thought, except he was afraid of swallowing more water.

James was bone cold and bone tired. He didn't know how much longer he could drag both of them through the cold, muddy, raging water. But he couldn't stop. He couldn't let Cady drown. And he couldn't let himself drown either.

At last the water was up only to his waist. He staggered against the force of the current, which threatened to knock him over and drag Cady away. With a last tremendous effort he lugged himself and Cady through the remaining yards of water.

They collapsed together on the shore. Cady coughed and moaned, and spat up once more. James just rolled onto his back and shut his eyes.

It was dark. How long had he been lying here? Had he slept until nightfall? He couldn't see the stars. Where was he?

James sat up. There was a blanket over him. He was in his family's wagon. How had he gotten here?

"Ma?" he croaked. His throat burned, and he had a terrible taste in his mouth.

Ma poked her head into the opening at the far end of the wagon. "Why, I see our sleepy young man finally woke up." She smiled at him. "Would you like something to eat? I have some nice corn cakes and molasses all ready for you."

James realized he was hungry enough to eat a mountain of corn cakes and a river of molasses.

A river. "Ma, where's Cady? Is she all right?"

"She's fine, Jamie. She's right beside you."

James looked over, and sure enough, there was Cady, asleep under the blanket.

"She's a little green from swallowing all that water, but she'll live. Thanks to you."

No wonder his throat hurt. He'd swallowed quite a bit of South Platte mud himself.

"Why isn't she in her own wagon?" James whispered.

A shadow passed over his ma's face. "I'm afraid Mrs. Walker is in no condition to take care of a sick little girl."

"But—" James started.

"That poor woman has enough on her hands with Scott being weak. She's not strong herself. And by the looks of her, I'd say there's more worries on the way." Ma gave James a look that said the subject was closed.

"How'd I get here?" he asked.

140

"Your pa and Mr. Walker rode after you. You and Cady were passed out on the bank. Two miles down-river, they said!"

"My land . . ." James murmured. It was hard to believe he'd been carried all the way back here without waking up. "Did everyone else make it okay?"

Again his ma looked troubled. "Mr. Loughery fell into the river when his horse stumbled. He hasn't been found yet."

James knew it could have been Cady and him.

Just then Mr. Walker appeared at the back of the wagon. "James. I'm glad you're awake. Everyone's been worried sick over you."

"I'm all right," he said modestly. He wished his ma would hurry with those corn cakes.

"You saved my little girl's life, James," Mr. Walker said. "I don't know how to thank you."

"Aw, you don't have to thank me," James said. His mother handed him a plate piled high with corn cakes smothered in molasses. He looked over at Cady. She was sleeping peacefully. "Just glad to be of help," he said between swallows.

# SEVENTEEN

## TWO CEREMONIES

"Ashes to ashes, dust to dust," said Colonel Stewart. He picked up a handful of soil and tossed it into the grave.

Mrs. Loughery wept quietly. Inside the hole lay her husband, wrapped in a simple wool blanket. There weren't enough trees on the banks of the South Platte to make a coffin out of.

James held his ma's hand and bowed his head. Mr. Loughery had been found that morning. He had washed up four miles downstream of the crossing place.

The colonel spoke quietly of the dangers of the trail, and of the terrible tragedy of a man's dying for his dreams. Mrs. Loughery stifled a sob.

The grave site was on a low knoll. A small breeze rustled the leaves of a cottonwood tree—the only one for miles around. The river, no longer swollen with rain but as brown as ever, wound its peaceful way nearby. A simple wooden cross would mark the spot. James thought it wasn't a bad place for a grave. Still, he was glad it wasn't his.

After asking the Lord to have mercy on the dead man's humble soul, Colonel Stewart said, "Amen." The people around the grave repeated the word after him.

Mrs. Loughery was crying openly now. Ma took her in her arms and led her down the hillock, murmuring words of comfort. James watched the other people follow them discussing broken wheel spokes and worn-out oxen. James knew their minds were already back on their own hardships.

Jeremy and Will picked up shovels and commenced throwing dirt back in the hole they'd just dug.

"Want me to help with that?" James asked.

"I can do it," Jeremy said, heaving a large pile of earth.

"Don't mind if you do," Will said, holding out his shovel. He winked at Jeremy. "Never break your own back if a man's willing to break his for you—that's what I always say."

Jeremy grunted, and he and James started shoveling.

Will flopped down in the shade of the cottonwood. He plucked a stem of grass and set it between his teeth. "The colonel gave a right fine sermon," he drawled, "wouldn't you agree?"

Neither James nor Jeremy looked up from his work.

"The colonel cuts a dignified figure," Will continued thoughtfully. "With that big feathered hat and that long yellow mustache. Doesn't he?"

James and Jeremy didn't respond.

Will sucked on the grass stem. "You can see why he's a colonel. And why he was elected leader of the train. He's like a wise old grandfather."

"He's not *that* old," James said between grunts.

"No. No, he's not old," Will allowed. "But he has a certain authority. Like a military officer should. Or like a minister."

"What're you goin' on about, Gantry?" Jeremy said, tossing aside his shovel. "What's all this nonsense about the colonel bein' a minister?"

"I didn't say he *is* a minister. I said he's *like* one."

"Well, what if he is?" Jeremy flopped down next to Will. James kept shoveling.

They were silent except for James's grunts of effort.

"I mean, the colonel performed the burial service," Will started up again.

"That's right. Who else was there to do it?" Jeremy asked.

"And, well, if the colonel can do funerals . . ." Will paused. "After all, the captain of a ship can perform marriages."

"*Now* what are you goin' on—" Jeremy started. "Wait a minute! You're not thinking what I think you're thinking, are you?"

James stopped shoveling. What was Jeremy thinking?

A slow grin crept across Will's face.

"You old dog!" Jeremy hooted, slapping Will across the shoulder with his hat. "Have you asked her yet?"

Asked who what?

"I sure have," Will replied. "Yesterday, just before the crossing."

"And she said yes?"

Will nodded. James noticed he was blushing. Will Gantry blushing! Now James knew he'd seen everything. But he still didn't understand what all the fuss was over.

"You asked her pa?" Jeremy said.

"Of course. He thinks it's a wonderful idea."

*What* was a wonderful idea?

"I can see it now." Will sighed. "Mrs. Sara Gantry."

"Mrs. Sara Gantry!" James blurted. "You're getting married?"

"Certainly," Will said. "What do you think we've been talking about?"

Jeremy and Will broke up laughing, and James joined them under the tree. The hole was about filled up anyway.

"I envy you," Jeremy said to Will. "I really do. If my Missy were here . . ."

James saw tears forming in his brother's eyes. Jeremy hadn't mentioned Missy in weeks. James had thought he'd forgotten all about her.

"You're young yet," Will said, placing his hand on Jeremy's shoulder. "I'm eighteen already. It's time I got settled. Maybe Missy will join you in Oregon someday."

"Maybe someday," Jeremy said morosely. It was obvious he didn't believe it. "But I don't want to spoil your happy occasion. Congratulations, Will. She's a fine girl."

"Yeah," James added. "Congratulations. Sara's prettier than a rosebud on a June morning."

Will shot him a suspicious look, then laughed good-naturedly. "That she is, James. That she surely is."

"Dearly beloved," Colonel Stewart began. "We are gathered here . . ."

Less than a week had passed since Mr. Loughery's funeral, and already the colonel was performing another ceremony. People were crying at this one too. But they were shedding tears of happiness, not of sorrow.

After long hours on the trail, the emigrants had formed the nightly circle in a small clearing not far from the river. They were due to reach Chimney Rock the next day. The sun was fast dropping out of

147

the sky by the time everyone was ready for the wedding.

Sara was in her Sunday best, a long sky-blue dress with lace around the sleeves and collar, and a stylish wide-brimmed straw hat. Her hair was tucked into a glossy fat bun on her neck, and she held a bouquet of wildflowers picked on the bank of the North Platte.

Will was in his Sunday best, too, though his weren't quite as nice—everything he owned fit in a saddlebag. He had on gray trousers, and a white shirt he'd borrowed from James's pa. It was a little big for him, but Will looked handsome anyway. The grand touch came from the beaver-pelt top hat Mr. Walker had lent him. Pierre Delaroux joked that it was an old acquaintance of his.

Will and Sara stood before Colonel Stewart in the center of the circled wagons. The colonel spoke of how everything had its season, of beginnings coming hand-in-hand with endings. Everywhere life and death were twined together, he said, and nowhere more so than on the trail.

James could hear Mrs. Loughery weeping softly. Then he saw Sara take Will's hand and hold it.

James nudged Cady. "They make a mighty fine couple, don't they?" he whispered. When she only sniffled in response, he glanced over at her. She was biting her lower lip to keep the tears from running down her cheeks.

148

He rolled his eyes and turned to Scott. James was going to say something about his blubbering sister when he noticed that Scott's eyes were filling up, too. He decided to keep quiet, and returned his gaze to Colonel Stewart.

"You may kiss the bride," the colonel concluded, and Will did just that.

Jeremy let out a whoop, and the party began.

The sky in the west was a brilliant, shattering red. It was the most spectacular sunset the emigrants had yet seen on the trail. Everyone commented on how nice it was that the weather had turned out so beautiful for Will and Sara's wedding.

Only Pierre Delaroux peered at the bloody sky disapprovingly. "I don't like it," he muttered. "Not one bit."

Pa dug his fiddle out of the back of the wagon, and he and several other fellows led reels and rounds, hornpipes and jigs, quadrilles and schottisches. Mr. Skonecki demonstrated the polka, and Mr. Moss even played a waltz or two on the concertina.

"Wanton harlotry . . ." James heard Mrs. Walker hiss at the couples holding each other tight and swaying through the waltz. Then she pinched up her face and stalked off to her wagon.

Mr. Walker, who was showing Cady the steps, started to go after his wife. Then he thought better of it and went back to Cady and the dance.

After staying in James's wagon for a couple of

days while she recovered from the near drowning, Cady had gone back to her family's wagon. James had been sorry to see her go. He knew she'd been happier with his family.

But he also knew Scott needed her. Mrs. Walker, Scott said, usually felt bad in the mornings and needed help breaking camp. But Scott was weak himself, and his father had to get the animals ready. Though she was only eleven, Cady was becoming mother to them all.

James watched Will and Sara swirling together among the dancers. He wondered if a girl as pretty as she would want to marry him someday. Then he saw Cady whirl by with her father.

He quickly put his mind on other things—such as the heaping plate of biscuits and fried pork his ma and the widow Loughery had just brought out.

# EIGHTEEN

## CHIMNEY ROCK

James awoke with a burning in his throat and a stinging in his nostrils. He blinked the grit out of his eyes and reached for his handkerchief to cover his face. The handkerchief was covered with dust.

In the tent beside him, Jeremy was coughing and groping for his own handkerchief. James crawled out of the tent. It was night, the blackest night he'd ever seen. The wind was blowing hard, but it wasn't a wet wind. The air was dry and gritty, and stung James's skin with every gust.

"Pa!" James called, stumbling through the darkness toward where he thought his folks' tent was. "Pa!"

"Jamie!" he heard over the wind. "Get in here, boy!"

James went in the direction of the voice. He

didn't see the tent until it was close enough to touch.

He dove through the flaps, into his pa's lap. "There's a dust storm out there you wouldn't believe!" he shouted.

"Is there now?" Pa said, chuckling. "Is Jeremy all right?"

Just then Jeremy burst through the tent flaps. "Am I glad to see you!" he exclaimed as he pulled himself off his pa and his brother. "I thought I'd never find you in all that dust."

"We were here the whole time," Elizabeth pointed out.

"You're right." Jeremy laughed, giving his little sister a gentle pinch. "How silly of me."

"Well," said Ma, "here we are. All together." She looked around at the bodies crammed into the little tent. All five of them were wearing handkerchiefs across their faces. They looked like a gang of robbers. "Isn't this cozy?"

That broke everyone up.

"I hope this storm is over by sunup," James said. "We don't want to lose any time on the trail."

"I'm afraid it's too late for that, son," Pa said. He reached into his overalls and pulled out his pocket watch. "It's past seven. Sun came up over an hour ago."

"What?" Jeremy exploded. "That can't be! It's pitch-black out there."

"It's the storm," said Ma. "There's so much dust

in the air, the sun can't shine through."

"Why'd you let us oversleep?" James asked. He couldn't believe he'd actually slept till seven. He must've done so because he'd been up late the night before, celebrating the marriage. He'd even danced with Sara.

"We're not going anywhere for the time being anyway," said Ma. "We'll just have to stay inside the tent and wait out the storm."

By five o'clock that afternoon, the storm still had not let up. If anything, it had gotten worse.

Even in the tent, the air was full of dust. It worked its way inside James's clothes; it made his eyes water; it made his tongue feel like sandpaper. His scalp itched, his joints ached from sitting down all day, and he was bored, bored, bored.

They'd played every game, told every joke, and asked every riddle they knew. They'd lit a candle so Ma could read aloud from *The Pilgrim's Progress*, which she always kept near her pillow. But her eyes watered so much, and her throat was so dry, that she couldn't read for long. They hummed and napped and listened to the wind howl. Finally they just sat staring glumly at one another in the dusty dark.

James was bored, bored, bored, and now he was hungry, besides. They'd had nothing to eat all day, and only the little water in his pa's bedside canteen to drink.

At last Pa announced he was venturing out. "The animals need to be fed and watered, and we need the same," he said. "I can't wait any longer."

"Do be careful, Sam," Ma said.

"And be sure to check on Bolt," James added.

Pa nodded and plunged through the tent flaps, disappearing into the black storm.

An hour later Pa tumbled back into the tent, coughing and sputtering. "Och," he said, "it's good to be out of that wind." His face around his handkerchief was bright red from the stinging dust.

"How're the animals, Sam?" Ma asked.

"Not happy, but unharmed," Pa reported. "I managed to feed and water all of 'em. Even Bolt," he added. "Or should I say, especially Bolt."

James smiled at his pa.

Pa opened the satchel he had slung over his shoulder and brought out some johnnycakes and jerky, along with a full canteen of water from the wagon.

While the others chewed on the hard biscuits and meat, Pa told of what he'd seen outside. "I ran into John Walker by his oxen."

James wondered momentarily what his pa was doing near the Walkers' oxen. Then he realized his pa must have been checking up on them.

"Seems all this dust is giving Scott trouble," Pa continued. He looked at Ma darkly. "Amelia's not doing too well either."

154

Ma shook her head. "That poor woman . . ." she said.

"John told me Pierre Delaroux'd said he'd been in a dust storm like this one once before. Lasted eight days."

Eight days! James was astonished. They would run out of water before then, and besides, he'd go crazy cooped up in the tent for another week.

"Mr. Delaroux said the thing to do is hit the trail," Pa went on. "We can't afford to lose a week of travel—snows come early to the western mountains. We don't want to end up like the Donners."

Only two winters before, the notorious Donner party had been stranded for months in the Sierra Nevadas. There were rumors that some in the party had eaten their dead companions to survive. James didn't fully believe the rumors, but the mere mention of the Donners shot fear into him.

"The storm came out of the west," Pa continued," so the faster we move that way, the faster we're out of it."

"But Sam, how can we go on if we can't see ten feet in front of us?" Ma asked.

"Colonel Stewart will ride the circle tomorrow morning and help us form the train. We'll be right behind the widow Loughery's wagon. She'll follow Will and the Jenningtons. The Walkers'll be behind us. Colonel Stewart and Mr. Delaroux will be at the head of the train, following the ruts of the trail."

Pa looked at each of the faces in the dark tent in turn. "If we stick to the ruts, and if everyone looks out for everyone else, we should have no trouble."

Dawn broke black as night. James had slept in his folks' tent alongside the rest of the family. They ate a quick breakfast of johnnycakes and water, then broke camp.

James, Jeremy, Elizabeth, and Ma piled into the wagon, where they were at least partially sheltered from the stinging dust. Pa wrapped as much of himself as possible in rags and kerchiefs. Only a narrow slit exposed his eyes. He waved to his family, then turned to go drive the oxen. He disappeared into the storm after only a step or two.

James and Jeremy took turns calling out to Mr. Walker, who was driving his oxen directly behind the Greggs' wagon. James could see only the lead pair; the oxen behind them were swallowed in the dust. Occasionally Mr. Walker would come into view. He was bundled up like James's pa.

It was a long, tiring day, and the train moved slowly. James could hear shouts coming from up and down the line—people calling to each other to let them know where they were. The widow Loughery sang hymns over and over for Pa to follow. It was nice in a way, but after the seventh rendition of "Savior, Like a Shepherd Lead Us," followed by the ninth of "Watchman, Tell Us of the

Night," James wished she would switch to hog calling or yodeling.

Bolt, along with Corncob and Mackie, plodded along next to the wagon on a short lead. He looked unhappy, but at least James knew he was safe.

Ma tried to keep their spirits up, but it was difficult. One time, when Elizabeth was on the verge of tears, Ma had to remind her that she was six years old and a big girl now. Elizabeth blinked back her tears and sat up straighter.

James and Jeremy grew testy. Neither one liked being stuck in the wagon all day. And in addition to the hymns from the front, from behind them they heard Mrs. Walker loudly reciting passages from the Bible: "'The Lord maketh the earth waste, and turneth it upside down. . . . The land shall be utterly emptied, and utterly spoiled: for the Lord hath spoken this word.'" She went on and on like that.

James thought even the widow Loughery's hymns were better than Mrs. Walker's predictions of doom.

And so the nightlike day ended and darker night fell. The emigrants didn't bother to form a circle. Who would attack them in a storm like this? The wind howled and the dust bit. And Pa estimated they'd traveled only a mile and a half.

The next day went much like the one before, except there was less shouting along the train. People's throats were so dry they could barely whisper. The widow Loughery stopped singing, and even Mrs. Walker could no longer be heard calling perdition down on their heads. The men driving the oxen depended more and more on the wheel ruts under their feet to keep them on course.

That night Pa had distressing news. "I hear tell the Sundstroms are missing," he told his family. The Sundstroms were a family of six; their wagon had been four behind the Greggs'. "One minute Harlan Teague is following their wagon. The next minute it's not there anymore. He called and called, but nobody answered, so he drove on up to the Batkins. They said Ulf Sundstrom had been right behind them. Then he and his wagon just vanished."

James shivered. He couldn't help thinking about the Sundstroms wandering alone in the dust storm, the wide plains all around them. They could drive unawares into a ravine, or get mired in the mud of the North Platte.

When would the hateful storm end?

The third day of moving, and the fourth of the storm, brought good news. The Sundstroms had found the wagon train. And now they were three wagons *in front* of the Greggs!

Pa told the story: "Ulf Sundstrom explained that they'd driven all night—in circles, he supposed. When morning came, he despaired of ever finding the train again. So he let the oxen pull the wagon in whatever direction they preferred while he napped in the wagon. They couldn't do a worse job than he'd done, he figured.

"Sure enough, not two hours later, his wife woke him up. She'd heard wagon wheels creaking directly ahead. The oxen had found their way back through the storm and saved them!"

Pa nodded. "Another example of the wisdom of beasts and little children."

"Little children?" Ma asked.

"Oh, I left that out. It was Sundstrom's little four-year-old daughter, Prudence, who told her daddy to let the oxen lead the way."

"Prudence?" Ma said. "Why, I do declare that child is well named!"

The next day disaster struck. The dust storm had shifted so much dirt around that sometime in the morning Colonel Stewart and Pierre Delaroux lost the wheel ruts. They'd kept moving forward, hoping to rejoin the trail, but by late afternoon it was obvious they were lost. It had been hours since anybody along the whole length of the train had seen the ruts.

"Maybe we should let Ulf Sundstrom's oxen lead us," Jeremy cracked.

No one laughed.

James knew that without the ruts or the sun to guide them, there was no way of telling what direction they were heading. They might have spent all day walking south. Or even east, back to where they'd come from. And though Colonel Stewart and Pierre Delaroux had traveled the route before, neither was very familiar with this part of the country.

Even after the storm ended, the emigrants might well be hopelessly lost. At best, it would take precious days to find the trail again.

James couldn't help thinking of the Donner party and its grisly end—too many days lost, and the Stewart party might suffer the same fate.

Dawn came. Dawn actually came. On the morning of the sixth day of the storm, a dull yellow glow appeared in the sky. And thankfully, the glow was behind the emigrants, in the east, which meant they were still traveling west.

The wind blew less hard and the air was less thick with dust. The train plodded forward. They were lost, but the people were visibly cheered. Even the animals were stepping higher. James saw his ma smile for the first time in days.

"We're gonna make it, Jamie," she said. "I just know we are."

Then James heard a sound coming from up ahead. It sounded like shouts—people whooping and hollering. Out of fear? Anger? Joy? The shouting rose, came nearer and nearer. James climbed out of the wagon for the first time in five days and squinted toward the front of the train. The dust stung his skin, but he didn't mind it.

He walked with the wagon, step after step, as he had for so many days, so many miles. Bolt was beside him, and then he was joined by Jeremy. Now Ma and even little Elizabeth were walking alongside him.

"What is it?" James asked.

Before anyone could answer, he heard the widow Loughery in the wagon ahead shout, "There it is! There it is!" It was the first sound she'd made since she'd stopped singing hymns.

Then James's pa, driving the oxen just twenty feet away, yelled, "I see it! Hoo-rah, I see it, too!"

James strode forward with the wagon, peering ahead, wondering what all the fuss was over. Finally he saw what the people ahead were shouting about.

A dark-red silhouette appeared dimly against the brackish yellow sky. It gained substance, then materialized out of the dust cloud to tower above them not half a mile away: the great cone base and soaring peak of Chimney Rock shimmered in the suddenly clear air.

"Chimney Rock!" James screamed, throwing his hat at the sky and ripping the handkerchief off his face. "Chimney Rock!"

The wagon train was on course after all. Colonel Stewart and Pierre Delaroux hadn't led the emigrants astray. They'd been slowed for several days

161

by the dust storm, but they weren't lost. Here was Chimney Rock thrusting its jagged pinnacle at the blue, blue sky, right where it was supposed to be. The first third of the journey was behind them.

James quietly repeated the words his ma had said to him earlier in the day. "We're gonna make it." Then louder, "We're gonna make it!"

The others picked up the cry, and soon it could be heard all up and down the wagon train.

Cady and Scott came running up from their wagon. They were skipping and shouting and throwing their hats in the air.

Pa dropped back to join his family in the celebration. The horses whinnied excitedly. Ma was laughing and crying all at once, and Jeremy couldn't stop whooping for joy. James picked up Elizabeth and hugged her. Then Jeremy and Ma gathered James and Elizabeth in a hug, and Pa wrapped his long arms around all of them.

The oxen plodded, the wagons rolled, and the Gregg family laughed and shouted and trotted along, all together, all safe, moving ever onward, ever westward.

*Here's a scene from the next*
*book in this exciting trilogy,*
Along the Dangerous Trail. . . .

Fort Laramie was a low, rectangular two-story structure with three blockhouses—two at opposite corners, and the third over the gate in the front wall. The fort had been built by the American Fur Company. The U.S. Army had little authority here on the frontier. American Fur Company agents ruled Fort Laramie like a private state.

Camped outside the fort was a group of Dakota Indians. They were tall and wore buffalo robes about their waists, but no paint. Their long black hair was pulled back and fixed in place with eagle feathers.

James had gotten used to seeing Indians along the trail. His family had traded with the Potawatomi. He, Cady, and Scott had even been saved from wolves by some Pawnee. But he was surprised to see Indians living so close to whites.

Then he remembered his pa had told him they were there to trade with the trappers, soldiers, and emigrants who passed through the fort.

James and Cady walked through the first of the two wide wooden gates. On the right was a little window in the adobe wall. Through it the people inside the fort could conduct business with the Indians while still keeping the inner gate closed. But today there was no threat from any Indian tribes. Both gates were wide open.

Inside, the fort was as crowded as Independence. There were blacksmiths and wheelwrights, trappers and traders. James and Cady couldn't believe the prices. A pound of flour cost fifty cents, as did a gross of fishhooks. Coffee, sugar, and salt were a dollar a pound.

What seemed like dozens of languages flew back and forth. Besides the fur company agents, soldiers, and emigrants who spoke English, there were Indians of every description, each using a different tongue, Mexicans talking in Spanish, and traders calling in French.

An elderly Oglalah Indian offered pemmican—dried buffalo meat ground up with berries, fat, and marrow. A Brulé Indian was hawking kinnikinnick, a variety of tobacco, and shongsasha, the bark of the red willow, also used for smoking.

Lining the walls of the fort were little rooms. Some were horse stables, and others, mostly on the second story, were quarters of the fur-company agents. Inside the upper rooms sat many Indian women, idly fanning at the dust and flies that choked the air.

Suddenly a commotion sprang up not far from where James and Cady were looking at a pair of beaded moccasins a Dakota wanted to trade. Quickly they made their way over to a crowd of men gathered in a corner of the yard. A number of them were shouting angrily and shaking their fists.

"What's all the fuss?" Cady asked James.

"Don't know," he answered. "Wait here." He recognized Mr. Teague among the men and sidled up to him.

"Mornin', Mr. Teague," James greeted him. "What're those men shouting about?"

"Why, howdy, James," said Mr. Teague. "Seems they caught the'selves a desperado in the Black Hills. That man over yonder." He pointed to the crowd. "They say he's been rustling horses. Him and his gang, the Clampson Boys."

"Land's sake . . ." James murmured. A real desperado. Back in Pennsylvania, he'd read stories about outlaws in the penny papers, but he never thought he'd see one. He stood on tiptoe and tried to peer over the backs of the men.

"They say the Clampson Boys is bloody murderous," Mr. Teague continued. "Shot some poor feller dead just afore we hitched out. In Independence."

"Independence?" James repeated. He'd seen a

shooting there. He'd fairly stepped over the wounded man.

"So they say." Mr. Teague nodded. "Though it warn't this one, but his brother that done it."

"What're they going to do with him?" James asked.

"Oh." Mr. Teague chuckled. "Them fellers'll invite him to a necktie party, I reckon."

James was about to ask Mr. Teague what he meant by that, but he'd disappeared into the crowd. James spotted Cady where he'd left her trying to get a look at what was going on.

He trotted over to her and repeated what Mr. Teague had told him. "What's a necktie party?" he concluded.

"A necktie party!" Cady whooped. "You don't know what a necktie party is? Hoo, you oughta thank your stars I know something about the world!"

James waited while Cady finished laughing. "All right, smarty," he said finally. "If you know so much, what *is* a necktie party?"

"A hanging!" Cady smirked. "If you weren't so blamed ignorant, you'd know that."

"Well, if you weren't so blamed ignorant," James retorted, "you'd know how to swim. I'm getting tired of saving your life all the time."

That calmed Cady right down. "Hmph," she said. "I can swim plenty. Just not in water over my head."

James laughed. "The river was only four feet

166

deep, and you nearly drowned in it." He waved his arms over his head. "Glug, glug, help me, help me," he teased.

It was true. Cady had nearly drowned in the raging waters of the South Platte River. James had risked his own life to rescue her.

Cady wrinkled up her face. "Never mind my swimming. Let's go watch the hanging. I hear tell they're mighty good entertainment." She grabbed his sleeve and led him toward the crowd.

The men were now gathered near a corner blockhouse. The blockhouse roof jutted past the fort's walls, extending into the yard at a height of about fifteen feet. Someone had tossed a rope over one of the roof's rafters. At the end of the rope dangled a noose.

James swallowed, and felt a tingling at the back of his neck. He sure wouldn't want that noose tied around him.

James could see the desperado now. The angry men had tied his hands behind his back and propped him up on a horse. He was a large man, with a long, narrow, bony face and deep-set eyes. By the looks of him, he hadn't had a meal in days. His clothes were raggedy and ill fitting, as if they'd been made for someone else, but his boots were shiny new. James shivered at the thought of where he'd gotten them— off a dead man's feet, no doubt.

Cady hadn't let go of his sleeve since she'd

dragged him over here, and now her fingers crept down around his own. He glanced over at her. She was staring at the proceedings with open mouth.

A man had climbed up on a barrel and was making a speech about how, as a representative of the American Fur Company, he was the law in these parts, and how he wasn't tolerating no horse-thieving scoundrels of any color.

James remembered a similar scene. A man in their wagon train, Jenson Carver, had shot and killed an Indian unprovoked. The emigrants had decided to hand him over to the Pawnees rather than risk reprisal. James knew that, despite this man's claims to be in charge, the will of the crowd was law on the frontier.

Swiftly the man on the barrel slipped the noose over the desperado's head. Someone else pulled the slack out of the rope and secured it to a hitching post.

Cady's grip on James's hand tightened.

*"Yah!"* the man on the barrel yelled, slapping the horse hard on the rear and leaping down from the barrel. The horse lunged forward a few steps, and the desperado tumbled off its back.

The desperado arched his body and kicked his legs out two or three times, swinging his bound arms behind his back. But the thrashing seemed only to tighten the noose around his neck.

He stopped kicking, and threw his head back tensely and gasped for air. A tight grimace creased his face. He was dangling three feet off the ground. His eyes blinked slowly in the noonday sun.

James's hand ached now, Cady was squeezing it so tight. But he paid it no mind. He was too caught up in the desperado's struggle for life.

The desperado made soft coughing noises between his clenched teeth. Gurgling noises rose from his throat. He started kicking again, thrashing around wildly, as if he were trying to swim in air. His body arched from the back of his head all the way down to his heels, then went limp. His face was a dark, dark red and was turning blue fast. He arched again, gurgling horribly.

James felt sick to his stomach. He'd seen men wounded before, but he'd never actually watched one die. He hadn't known how awful it would be.

Now, too, his hand was hurting him badly. Cady's nails were digging into his skin. He looked at her. A tear was running down her freckled cheek, and she looked pale. James regretted watching the necktie party. He wanted to leave. But somehow he couldn't help staying till the last dance was done.

The desperado arched one more time and went limp. His head flopped forward, chin on collarbone, tongue on lower lip. He blinked ever so slowly, once, twice, and then his eyes stared ahead dully, seeing nothing, saying nothing.

It was over.